The Story of James

and Other Writings

The Story of James

and Other Writings

FRANKLIN LAFAYETTE KING

*t*P
Texture Press
2014

This book is a work of fiction. Names, characters, businesses, organizations, places, events, and incidents either are the product of the author's imagination or are used in a fictitious manner. Any resemblance to actual persons, living or dead, events, or locales is entirely coincidental.

Published in the United States by
Texture Press
1108 Westbrooke Terrace
Norman, OK 73072

For ordering information,
visit the Texture Press website at
www.texturepress.org

ISBN-13: 978-0-692-31702-0
ISBN-10: 0692317023

Cover painting by Franklin L. King

Book design by Arlene Ang

Table of Contents

Poetic Moments

Inspiration from the Impressionists

Poems and Other Thoughts

Snippets of Thoughts

The Story of James

To
James

So long as men can breathe or eyes can see,
So long lives this, and this gives life to thee.

Shakespeare, "Sonnet 18"

The Story of James

Could I have felt such love before?
That which destroys now builds anew.

I think not of what is to be.
Only a fool plans beyond the day.

It is the laugh that I seek.
A place to hide within your smile.

CHAPTER 1

Metamorphosis

JOHN JOHNSON'S FLIGHT LEFT BOSTON LOGAN AIRPORT fifteen minutes late. As was his habit, he had arrived at the airport much too early for the scheduled departure. He needed time to relax, to think in the presence of the indifferent. He thumbed through magazines without any intention of purchasing one. Then he entered a café and ordered a cup of coffee. There he sat, as an artist might, observing those about him.

A few hours later, he looked out the window at the towering clouds that floated silently above the land. Sooner than expected, the plane began its descent. As he looked down upon the sprawling city beneath him, he thought of the transcendentalist that said, "City life. Millions of people being lonesome together." Those words from a nearly forgotten class of English literature haunted his emotions. He put his seat in an upright position and waited for the wheels to touch ground.

It rained in Houston the day John arrived. The dark clouds, a curtain separating the earth from the light above. To him, Houston was a city of cancer. It did not matter that Rice University, a premier citadel of higher education, and the Museum of Fine Arts were located near the clinic. He was coming to Houston for only one reason: to live.

After arriving at Hobby Airport and taking his luggage from the carousel, John rented a small white SUV. He adjusted the mirrors in the car and looked at himself in the reflective glass. He did not recognize the person staring back at him. He quickly looked away from the image before him: the thinning face, the dark circles beneath the eyes.

As he drove down Interstate Highway 610 West, he first thought that the skyline of the Southwest Comprehensive Cancer Center, with its small skyscrapers, was the city of Houston. The Cancer Center's tall metallic buildings pierced the low bulbous clouds that covered the northern horizon.

It was to him, a place where the pathetic, the unmentionables of modern society, congregated to await the inevitable. Now he too had joined the community of the misbegotten. He was bitter that cancer had stricken him for no apparent reason. "Bitter" – yes, that was the word. It was true that he had lived too fast and too hard, but his youthfulness should have been his savior, a preventive against a disease reserved for old age. John had never thought about the nature of cancer or the toll it took on others. He had created about him an impenetrable field that nothing, not even love, could pass through.

In Boston when former friends greeted him before his departure, they looked at him as though he were an object of medical curiosity. When a casual acquaintance recognized him at Logan Airport, he put his arm around John and said, "My, you don't seem to have lost any weight, your color is still good." Perhaps the comment that disturbed him the most was "You look so good." Never before had virtual strangers made such remarks.

"Am I not the same person?" John thought. "No," he confessed to himself, "I am not."

His cancer reflected a mirror image of John's inward struggle. He had failed to appreciate the intelligence and the survival skills of a disease that was, by its very nature, his own self. His body now consisted of two cell types, the good and the bad. The bad cells he had created within him were now destroying him. His T-cells, those sentinels of defense, were unable to recognize that which was so apparent to any oncologist. The doctors could do nothing to stop the foe's progress. Only his death could halt the army of invaders.

John had always managed to stay a safe distance from tragedy. He believed that by not sharing or becoming involved in other people's lives, he could remain both safe and content. He often quoted Henry David Thoreau: "I love to be alone. I never found the companion that is so companionable as solitude." It was his own isolation that both defined and momentarily comforted him.

WHEN FIRST DIAGNOSED WITH THE ILLNESS, he had returned home. He had earlier received his commission as a Naval Officer after graduating from Texas A&M. His mother had insisted that he attend her alma mater, Boston College, but he rebelled. He had dreamed of being a career naval aviator, but due to a vision problem became a shipboard officer aboard a destroyer. After serving the required four years, he entered the civilian world without a clear vision of what he wanted to be. His father, a doctor in Boston, encouraged him to attend law school. Since his father had combined the highly lucrative fields of law and medicine, he felt that his father's advice possessed a degree of merit. "There is nothing as conspicuous," said his father, "as wealth."

John was unusually handsome with his thick, black hair and unusual green eyes. He stood over six feet and had the body of a runner. Being athletic, he was considered an up-and-coming tennis player at the country club where his family belonged. While women immediately noticed him, he had little interest in them after his passionate affair with Edna had ended. He had been too close to the flame and gotten badly burned.

After his tour in the Navy, he studied law and directed his passions towards his sailboat and the sea. Every free moment was spent polishing the brightwork, caulking seams and painting his beloved 1927 forty footer. His life was, therefore, carefully balanced between his studies and his avocation as a sailor.

On the open ocean, he felt most alive and in control. If a storm approached, he knew exactly what to do. Fear was not a part of his nature. The stronger the wind, the more exhilarated he felt. He loved it when the railing knifed through the swells as water fled through the scuppers.

Weeks before graduating from law school, he noticed himself getting weaker. Even though he continued to occasionally sail in the harbor with only a few ventures into the Atlantic, he needed to sit down more and more. After sailing one day, he found himself falling in front of the fountain in his family's walled garden only to be awakened by the sting of an insect perched on his exposed arm.

"Perhaps it's a lingering cold," he thought to himself. The last semester had been a difficult one and paying the temporary price of good health was not uncommon to the ambitious. Like many highly sought-after goals, academics had become uncommonly stressful. However, with his family's encouragement and his father's financial support, he persisted until graduation.

His internist, after a complete physical examination, encouraged him to see an oncologist. Almost immediately, the doctor identified the problem. Without immediate medical attention, the physician said, "Perhaps six months, a year with treatment. This type of cancer is very unpredictable. I would suggest taking some time off and just enjoying life. You know, none of us have forever." When John heard the prognosis, he immediately felt numb. Small beads of perspiration formed on his forehead while his mouth became dry. So dry that he found it too difficult to swallow. At that moment, John was unable to form the most elementary of words.

He immediately left the medical complex in Boston and drove his BMW to his family house on the outskirts of the city. As the gates to his family's estate opened, he felt the irony of the situation: a new law degree, some thoughts on attending medical school, and now cancer.

He drove up the winding drive to the large brick Tudor-style house that sat among an ancient grove of chestnut trees. After parking his car near the main entrance to the house, he left the engine running and got out. In his anxiety, he didn't even hear Phillip say, "Sir, your mother and father are waiting for you in the library."

He looked at Phillip as though he were an apparition in the dim light of the richly wooded foyer. "What was that?"

"Sir, your mother and father are awaiting you in the library."

John had called shortly after his meeting with his doctor, but did not describe what had transpired at Boston General. He only told his mother that he needed to speak to them both about an urgent matter. As he walked into the paneled library with its fine collection of books, leather chairs and mahogany desk, his mother rose to greet him. His father put down the *Wall Street Journal* on his desk and stared at him as though his arrival were merely a casual interruption.

"Son, your mother said you sounded a bit concerned on the phone," said his father. "How can we help you?"

John did not know how to respond. Should he be blunt and quickly sum up the horror of his situation or should he cloak it in terms of optimism and a possible misdiagnosis? He paused before responding, then quietly said, "I have cancer, a particularly bad type. Dr. Myers told me that I have the lifespan of a small animal, more or less."

Ironically, when John was a young boy, he read that his new pet would only live a hundred days. The gerbil had been very healthy and could chew paper rolls throughout the night until it died. Then when the hundredth day of its life arrived, the gerbil suddenly died just like the book on animals said it would.

Even though his father had been a brilliant physician, now he only concentrated on malpractice suits that yielded a far greater profit. The compassion of healing had long since passed from him. He arose and, rather than embracing John, took his hand as though to shake it, "John, I can't give you any better medical advice than to go to Houston for treatment." His father was a native Texan and when young, had several classmates that later worked at the world-renowned Cancer Center located just south of the city central.

John felt that regardless of where he traveled, the results were going to be the same. He knew he would be told the same thing: "There is no cure. All we can promise you is that we will treat the disease. If we treat the cancer, you will have a year or so. If not, only a few months. We can promise, however, to make you comfortable with palliative care at the end."

John had read about miracle cures. The man who outlived his doctor by returning to Greece and resuming his native habits: drinking red wine, dancing, and laughing through the moments of his disease. "Good reading but nothing more," he reasoned to himself. John knew the enemy lived inside him, fed upon him, and would in time conquer his desire to live. John remembered a high school friend with leukemia who told him, "If this is living, I don't want to live." John recognized once more that when hope is lost, life ceases.

He also recalled the words of his grandmother as she lay dying in the upstairs bedroom of her home in New Port, Rhode Island, "John, I am just tired. Just very, very tired." Those were the last words she had spoken to him. Like John, her doctors had not given her any encouragement. Her will to live had simply ceased. She never uttered the sentiments of Dylan Thomas, addressed in secret to his dying father:

> *Do not go gentle into that good night,*
> *Old age should burn and rave at close of day;*
> *Rage, rage, against the dying of the light.*

FOR THE NEXT FEW WEEKS, JOHN SLEPT LATE in his large bedroom on the northeast corner of the second floor of his parent's home. Diplomas, ribbons, and other awards that constituted, at least to his parents, the high marks of his life graced the walls of his bedroom. As he lay in bed, he thought about the meaninglessness of all that he saw before him. What good had his life been, what purpose had it served?

Neither he nor his family believed in God or in any type of spiritual practice. His mother was raised a Catholic and by tradition, she would remain one. Throughout her adult life, she treated her faith as a political organization: who to vote for and why.

When John was very young, he thought his mother's fixation on yoga was based on her religious beliefs. Her obsession demanded that everyone in the family adhere to a schedule that worked around her sessions. It was the unending news and stock reports that constituted the rituals of his father's time.

When he visited his parents' friends, their families often said a blessing before the meal especially at holiday times of the year. When he asked his father why his family never prayed, his father responded, "You are only praying to yourself. No one hears you but your own conscience. We are no more than field mice, living, struggling, and dying just like they do."

ONE MORNING AFTER HIS DIAGNOSIS, JOHN WENT DOWN to the local coffee shop. There he ordered a large mocha. Seating himself at a corner table, he picked up a discarded magazine. On the cover, it read, "Cancer Breakthrough." John then read where one of the world's foremost experts on his particular disease practiced in Houston. It had never occurred to him how many others were affected by the same cancer. While only a few in the States had his particular type, worldwide the numbers were astonishing.

Upon returning home, he quickly went to his computer and searched the category of online appointments in Houston. Perhaps his father was right, even though he did not want to admit it, for he had always resented his father's interference in his life. Yet in the end, his father had always been correct.

After filling in the form, he pressed the submit key on his laptop. In less than a day, the cancer center acknowledged his request for an appointment. His initial visit was scheduled for the following week. He immediately sought an alternative date since he could not possibly arrive there within such a short period of time.

He decided to rent a temporary apartment in which to live during his search for a resolution to his illness. To be honest, he was tired of searching for a cure or, at best, a brief extension of his life. Yet he knew that doing nothing would not be the answer for him. John was determined not to go gently into that good night.

He wanted something comfortable to live in and yet close to the cancer center. After sending numerous e-mails, he was informed that an apartment would be available upon his arrival. Wendy, the property manager, assured him that all he needed to bring was the proverbial "toothbrush."

As he entered the parking lot of his new apartment, he looked at the well-kept brick building, each room with a small balcony. After getting the key from Wendy, John struggled with his luggage up the stairs to his apartment on the third floor. He could not believe that there was not even an elevator. As he laboriously climbed the stairs under the weight of his luggage and with the laptop computer slung over his shoulder, a young woman in shorts ran past him skipping every other step on her way up. In some ways, he was glad to see her youthful energy. Even though he had only a brief glance at her, she radiated both good physical health and happiness.

As he breathed heavily, John thought to himself, "I suppose many of the people who live here don't need an elevator. Since both the hospital and Rice University are nearby, this must be a place where medical residents live while completing their studies. Thank goodness I don't have to see sick people, I am depressed enough."

John's room was basic: a living and dining room combination, one bedroom, kitchen and bath. The utility room had both a washer and dryer. Outside the French doors, he could hear ambulances passing and the sounds of unending traffic congestions. He quickly learned when the workforce arrived for work and when they fled

Houston for the suburbs that expanded almost daily towards the island of Galveston.

The apartment complex was gated with multiple combinations to the various entrances and exits. The tall, black picket fence with dull spears at the top ensured that the desperate of the city did not enter the complex. Like all experienced nomads, he instinctively sensed what streets were safe and what alleyways should be avoided.

He stretched forth his large calendar on the coffee table and studied the dates of his medical appointments. He then highlighted the schedules with various colored markers indicating the status of their relevancy. He did not write anything else on the calendar.

John was reluctant to share his experiences with family and friends. In fact, he did not want to hear from anyone. He, however, denied what was so apparent within him: he desperately wanted people to care.

After a sleepless night in which he managed to remember several much-needed items he had forgotten at home, he arrived for his scheduled appointment. The large medical complex was not easy to navigate. The online map with driving instructions was printed far too small to be read from the driver's seat.

After finding the correct elevator among many in the main building, he seated himself within view of a huge saltwater aquarium. A large puzzle with only the edges put together sat on a table. The yellow, blue and red tropical fish of various sizes swam slowly within the manmade Eden. He thought about how safe and limited their world was. Both fear and knowledge had been removed in their small aquatic world of salt water and artificial plants.

John did not want to see the other patients waiting for their fortunes to be told. By the very nature of the clinic title, he knew that very little hope would be offered to them and to himself as well. From his Internet readings, he thought about the various lab animals in the clinical studies that managed to survive their illnesses due to some new drug. Yet that miracle drug never seemed to make it into human studies.

While sitting there, an older man with thinning gray hair and dark brown eyes looked at him. "What you doing here young man? You are not old enough to be in this waiting room," he said loudly. John did not react to his comment. After a pause, the elderly man continued, "Life isn't fair, is it?" Without waiting for a reply from John, he answered his own question, "No, it isn't. Got cancer and didn't even smoke. Did nothing wrong I guess. I even went to church. My wife says she always prayed for me even when I didn't. Makes you wonder, don't it?"

After looking away as though expecting an answer from the ether, the older man continued, "I reason that it doesn't matter what we do, we still get sick."

John did not want to engage in conversation. He did not want to talk to the mirrored image of himself. John deliberately did not respond. Instead he watched the slow moving fish as though viewing them through a child's kaleidoscope.

The stranger tried again to solicit John's attention. "I think it was related to my rating in the Navy and later on to my job in the oil fields. A man's body can only take so many synthetic things. Nothing pure in the environment anymore. The assholes knew what the jobs would eventually do to me. Neither the Navy nor the goddamn oilfields gave a damn about long-term health effects."

"I agree. Not many governments or corporations give a shit," replied John. He too had been exposed to those "synthetic" things while serving aboard ship.

"Do you think that God cares?" asked the older man.

"Don't know. Haven't heard from him," replied John.

"Yeah, me neither." With that comment, the inquisitor turned around and faced the elevators. John was thankful he had not fallen into a theological discussion, particularly a debate. He did admire the man for his honesty and quickly sensed the hopelessness in his voice.

As John looked around, he was surrounded by people from around the world. A wealthy Saudi gentleman was dressed in full-length white apparel consisting of the taqiyah, ghutra and igal. The exquisite nature of his clothing indicated a man of wealth and influence. A Mexican family's children played freely among the patients' feet, pushing small plastic toys on the carpeted floor. The little girl occasionally smiled at John while her younger brother only frowned at him.

A mother and daughter from South America appeared somber. He could understand a few of their words thanks to a Spanish class he had taken online while serving in the Navy. They did not attempt to mask their fears or concerns for the man they had accompanied that day to the clinic. He was called to the back with an interpreter and the doctor's nurse led him to a small cubicle. There alone and afraid, he waited for the doctor.

Soon John's name was called. His legs felt weak as he walked with a young nurse to be weighed and have his blood pressure taken. He questioned the relevancy of having his measurements taken when it was so obvious he was dying inside. His grandfather had often said, "Pneumonia and heart attacks are an old man's best friends." John at this moment agreed with the elder Mr. Johnson: "Fast and clean is what I need."

The doctor walked in and fumbled with the cubicle's computer. The nurse that followed him quickly worked her charm on the reluctant machine that blinked several times before steadying upon the clinical images that followed. The doctor reviewed silently the PET/CT scan. John was seated too far back from the screen to see the details clearly.

The doctor then pushed himself back from the computer screen and extended his hand while holding a clipboard in the other. "Mr. Johnson, I am Dr. Caldwell. It is nice to see you." Immediately he continued, "It seems that you have been to several doctors before. They seem to agree on the status of your disease. However, I want to order some more tests. As you know we not only see patients, but we also engage in a great deal of research that frequently results in clinical trials that could be of some benefit to you."

John thought once more of the rodents that were cured from the myriad clinical trials they had involuntarily participated in. John then looked at Dr. Caldwell. "But I have already had enough tests."

The doctor looked sternly at him. "Not in this hospital. You haven't undergone the tests you need."

"Okay, do what you will. I assume that insurance will continue to pay for the same thing over and over."

The doctor only smiled in reply.

More CT scans, more bone marrow biopsies, more blood tests, more chest x-rays, more blood extractions. To John, it was all the same. With each test, he became increasingly tired while the feeling of despair grew inside him. It was like being told, "Guess what, it's raining!" when you had water dripping from your clothes.

Three days later, he received a phone call. "The doctor would like to see you. Please check the date and time of your appointment through our secure website." John did not question the faceless voice that dictated the commands so clearly.

When he arrived for his appointment, the doctor looked seriously at John. "I must concur with the findings of the other doctors. However, there is a clinical trial involving proton radiation. Would you be willing to participate?"

"Let's see, if I don't, I will die. If I do, I will die. Okay, why not? If it will make the medical profession happier."

Dr. Caldwell only smiled. "I will have to leave you now. I have seven more patients waiting," the doctor said as he abruptly left the room. John noticed the time. It was after five.

"Autistic asshole," said John to himself.

IT WAS A HOT DAY IN HOUSTON, TEXAS. A duplicate of the preceding one. As John entered the treatment center, he was greeted by a friendly, yet professional young woman. "How can I help you today, sir?"

"Hey, I am nearly your age, you can really drop the 'sir' routine," said John.

"Yes, sir. What is your MRN?"

"My what?" asked John implying, as a token of humor, that he had no idea what she was talking about.

"You're Medical Record Number," she replied. "It's on the bracelet you were issued the other day. You know, your first visit here. It's an important number. You need to memorize it."

"Is it as important as your phone number?" he asked with a smile.

"Sir, may I see your bracelet?" She then entered the number into her computer and asked him to proceed to the basement floor.

He walked towards the long winding stairs. Below, a large fountain could be heard splashing water against synthetic stone. As

John peered from the top of the staircase, he noticed some people sitting around talking to one another while others were alone resting their heads on the backs of fake leather chairs. Everyone appeared to be waiting as though they were about to board a Southwestern flight.

Many of the older men carried bottles of water – an indication of prostate cancer. John, however, noted that several were younger than he would have expected. "No age discrimination here," he thought. "The prostate gland waits for no man."

He did not take the elevator down for it would indicate he was too sick to use the stairs. "Strangely," he thought to himself, "I feel fine. Those lying sons of bitches back in Boston must have gotten my medical record confused with some old bastard." As John continued his journey down the stairs, he knew better.

He carried his bottle of FIJI water with him since he had walked to the Center from his temporary housing location just a few blocks away. He hoped that no one would confuse him with the prostate cancer patients. Even though he was dying, he still considered himself a good catch.

He nervously picked up a discarded magazine that featured prominent Houston doctors and their contributions to the medical field. "No more of this propaganda for me," he said to himself as he dropped the magazine loudly on the table. He then began to observe the other people. Like himself, he referred to them as 'victims.'

There, next to the entrance of the treatment facility, sat a young woman alone. Beside her was a red stroller. He knew all too well what that meant. John, while waiting, had seen several young children enter the two adjacent swinging doors. The children looked so small and frail. Many of them did not have hair to cover their large cranial scars. A mother carried a baby through the two doors in what appeared to be a wicker basket. Surrounding the mother was her family and friends wearing T-shirts that read MELANIE'S TEAM.

The young woman who sat alone by the swinging doors was beautiful with her blond hair tied in a ponytail. She was scanning a magazine far too quickly, which indicated she was nervously looking at the pictures with little or no intent to read the accompanying articles.

An older man carrying a large sack approached the young woman and sat down beside her. She managed a smile, but remained aloof. He looked towards John, without acknowledging his presence. Judging from the distance between the two, it was apparent they did not know one another. John thought to himself, "That old fart is going to flirt with her." After a brief conversation, the old man placed the sack in her lap and smiled at her as he spoke. John could not hear what he was saying.

He could not help but think of Tennessee William's Blanche DuBois when she said: "I have always depended on the kindness of strangers."

As the young woman waited, her fingers nervously tapped the metal table next to her. She took a drink from a lipstick-stained Styrofoam cup. Suddenly the doors swung open and two nurses appeared. The male nurse in his spotless blue uniform was carrying a small child who was still asleep under anesthesia. John reasoned that small children had to be kept still in order to receive the power of the beam with its high degree of accuracy. It was a paradox: a killing beam of energy that could save a child's life.

The mother took the infant from the nurse's arms and kissed his forehead. The child remained listless in her arms. After she returned to her seat, the small toddler began to stir. With the gradual return of the little boy's consciousness, she picked up her purse with her other hand and attempted to collect the sack that had been left.

John immediately got up and walked over to her. "May I help you carry some of your things?"

She looked at him for a moment as though questioning the intent of his offer. After a moment she said, "That would be nice. As you can see, I don't seem to be able to manage everything." They walked towards the elevator.

On the way up, John asked the small awakening child, "What is your name?" The toddler attempted to answer, but his words were inaudible.

"His name is James," the mother said. "He is not able to speak clearly now. He is still drowsy from the anesthetic. On his next birthday, he will be four."

John pretended to carry on a conversation as though the little boy was listening attentively to him. "Well James, my name is John. It looks like we are two of the twelve apostles," he said as he turned towards the young mother. "Your son has a noble name."

"Oh, I am sorry, my name is Karen Nicholson." She paused for a moment. "I don't know what I was thinking of. I don't usually give my full name to a stranger."

"You can't call me a stranger since we have so much in common," responded John.

She looked at him quizzically, then said, "Oh I understand, you are here as a patient. I should have known."

After opening the swing door of her older-model white SUV, he paused to help her load James into his seat. John noticed the large scar on the back of his head. He immediately looked away. "I hope that both of you have a great weekend. I assume he does not have any treatments on Saturday."

"That's right. It is just James and me now. We are free to do what we want to on weekends." Her words did not convey any nuances of flirtation or expectation. It was like the call of a young bird perched on a high branch who knew that it must fly alone regardless of what would occur next.

"Your husband is not with you?"

"No. After James was diagnosed with neuroblastoma, my husband left us. He had been planning it for several months. Apparently, a co-worker offered him something we couldn't. What about you? Is your wife with you?"

"No, I am afraid not. You see, I am still single. I am twenty-eight, and I figured that I would get to enjoy a few more years of bachelorhood before settling down with a family. Funny, sometimes things don't work out the way you intend them to." With those words, he turned and walked towards his treatment session.

Glancing back, he said, "I tell you what, I plan to go to Galveston next Saturday. I used to live there as a child. Why don't you two come with me? I will even treat you to a cottage by the sea. A friend from law school has loaned me his beach house for the weekend. He said that usually only sea rats stay there and I was more than welcome to it."

Karen smiled at his lack of pretention. After a thoughtful pause, she said, "I don't even know you."

"I tell you what, I will give you my medical record number for positive identification." He extended his arm out to her so she could read the number on his hospital-issued plastic bracelet. "I guess this is not too impressive for a first date?" John laughed.

"Besides, I assume our schedules are similar. If they are, you can decide after a week."

"Let me think about it." As she backed her SUV, she waved at him. From the backseat, James slowly turned his head towards John. He did not see a smile, only an awakening stare of recognition.

John reentered the building and proceeded down the stairs to the waiting room. Shortly afterwards he was called to the changing room. There he put on two gowns. One to cover the back of his body, the other to cover the front portion. Soon he was called to enter what seemed to be a concrete bunker, lit as though he were the guest speaker at a convention preparing to emerge on stage. After passing the last sharp corner, he found what looked like a gurney before him.

"Mr. Johnson, let me see your MRN," said the friendly voice of a technician. John turned his arm so she could see the number. "This will not take long. Just remember to lie very still."

THAT NIGHT, HE RETURNED TO HIS APARTMENT. Even though he watched the news and started a Red Box movie, a deep sense of loneliness came over him. He started to call his mother, but knew that his father would not approve of such a sign of weakness. His friends' lives continued on towards meeting their professional goals and extending their bloodlines.

He stared at the darkening street outside the French doors. At first he attempted to calculate the flow of traffic on the street but soon gave up since the rush to escape Houston was too great for him to calculate. Instead he was content to watch a small bird on the branch of a red crape myrtle just outside the patio. He had seen crape myrtles in California while stationed in San Diego, but never one as large or as beautiful as the ornate tree before his window. The small finch looked at him inquisitively. Even when John approached the patio doors, it did not fly away. "I must remember to get some bird food. At least I now have a companion."

The next morning, John awoke early and went down to the recreation room. He used to enjoy the communal experience of people exercising together, but now the gym-like smell bothered him. For a while he had the pleasure of having the room all to himself. Eventually other people joined him, mounting the equipment without speaking. An unspoken competition seemed to consume the room as everyone increased the speed and incline elevation of their machines. He had planned on using the workouts to gage his physical condition. Now he began to experience the fatigue of his illness and its treatment.

Every day he worked out, he became increasingly tired. Instead of watching television later in the evenings, he would go to sleep only to awaken in a pool of night sweat. He wondered if he should give up on a cure, accept what lay ahead, and cease to rage against the dying of the light.

Food quickly became bland and tasteless. He longed for a strong drink, but he knew it would only irritate his damaged organs. There was nothing left for him, nothing at all.

Each day he arrived early for his treatment but did not see Karen or James. Perhaps their schedule had been changed. Though very disappointed, he inwardly felt embarrassed about asking a stranger to spend the weekend with him. In the past when he was a naval officer, such an offer meant getting drunk and laid in the same evening – nothing more. Now it seemed like he was two people, the past and the present. There was no future person inside him.

FRIDAY ARRIVED. OR SO HE THOUGHT because the passage of the sun dictated the measurement of time. While waiting to be called for his treatment, a patient seated next to him asked how he was enjoying Houston. While it was only small talk, it helped get his mind off what was occurring.

"Houston? Oh yes, Houston. Fine," he responded.

"By the way, I am Bud, Bud Rountree. I see you in here every day. I hope things are going well for you."

"Yeah, my name is John Johnson. You would have thought my family could have come up with a better combination for a name."

"Well at least it is easy to remember. I know the unspoken rule: Never ask a fellow patient what he is doing here or how he is feeling. We all know."

"Yeah, you are right," replied John hoping that their conversation would be brief.

"When I retired, I thought about moving to Mexico. Then a friend laid it on the line and told me that when a fellow retires to Mexico, at first his children and friends come to visit him. But by the time he dies, no one bothers to attend his funeral. The Mexicans have to take care of him themselves. I got to thinking about what he said. I figure what he told was true. Of course when you are dead, who gives a shit who attends your funeral?"

John saw his own reflection in the eyes of his fellow patient. They both fell silent as they waited for their treatments.

John's treatment went quickly that day. The proton beam did its job without a hitch. His skin was beginning to be reddened by the rays, very much like a sunburn.

His main concern now was what to eat. John knew that if he ate what he wanted to, it would probably make him sick. There were two side effects that he did not want from radiation: fatigue and diarrhea.

As he started up the winding stairs, he looked down to see the doors of the treatment center swing open. Karen emerged, carrying James who was still asleep from his treatment session, his head red from the radiation. She looked up and smiled at him.

John stopped and began descending the stairs. As if by instinct, he reached out and took James. The small body was cooler than he thought it should be. He held James close to his chest as he would his own child. For a moment, John felt that this was his own family, then he remembered that it was a stranger's family.

Karen looked at him. "John, I know this is crazy and somewhat risky for all of us, but we accept your offer to go to Galveston. James did not know what Galveston was until I explained to him that it was an island where fish swim and birds fly freely. A place that is warm and safe. Sort of like his being in your arms now."

CHAPTER 2

A Safe and Warm Place

Early the next morning John picked up Karen and James at the Ronald McDonald House. James was still sleepy from having just eaten breakfast. During weekdays, he was not allowed to eat before his afternoon treatment. Saturday morning was different – he had awakened early and was very hungry.

Karen could not remember a time before when he had eaten all of his specially prepared breakfast and asked for a bite of her pancake. It was as if she had been told that he was better, that their morning was going to be a normal one, like what other people share as a family. It was a moment in which she felt happiness emerge. She had to be cautious with her feelings for no doctor had ever offered her any hope for a cure. Yet like words in a silent prayer, she could not contain the feeling of happiness that the morning brought her. She knew that her joy was a result of John arriving to take them to a different place where they could laugh and James could play even if only in his imagination.

"John, I am really happy. It seems like it is the first time I have been happy in many days." As she spoke, she turned to watch James sitting in his stroller. He looked up at her and smiled. In his small hand, he held the dinosaur that the old man at the Center had given him. In his other hand was a wooden toy with a smiling face – a gift from his father just before he left.

"As long as James is awake, he will not put the train engine down. I think he really longs for his dad. He never says it, but I can tell. It is too bad his father never put him first. James is the most special thing in the world to me. You would think his father would have felt the same way. I can understand his being indifferent to me, but why James? What did he ever do to him?"

"You know, Karen, seeing you and James together shows me just how much I have missed. Sometimes we don't get a second chance to know what is important."

Karen smiled. "We all get them. We just aren't aware of it most of the time."

INTERSTATE 45 IS ONLY FORTY-SEVEN MILES TO GALVESTON. It is a straight highway devoid of any scenery except for the small marshes alive with water birds. Cranes with their long legs could be seen fishing in the shallows. Seagulls circled above the marshy land that stretched towards low hanging summer clouds that rode upon the southerly Gulf wind.

The waters of the marshes reflected the colors of the sky. At times a brilliant blue, at others the shadows of clouds would turn the waters into mirrors that reflected the dark sky.

As they neared Galveston, James took delight in pointing towards the marshy ponds and the clouds above them. John pretended to have a great interest in his delightful discoveries of birds and shapes within the summer clouds. James' language consisted more of signing rather than spoken words.

"Karen, you must have taught him elementary sign language. He is excellent at communicating what he wants without talking."

"I am afraid the tumor may have affected his hearing. I really don't know at this point. They do not want to test him until after his radiation treatment. I learned sign language in high school since one of my best friends was deaf."

"You are one up on me there. I never really learned anything practical in school. Full of dates and names but little else."

"John, you have been very successful as a naval officer and now you are an attorney. My being a schoolteacher looks very insignificant in comparison."

"Karen, what could be more important than affecting the lives of children?"

"You are very nice to say that. Having James has been my greatest accomplishment in life."

Soon they were crossing the large bridge that connected the mainland to the island. James became very excited as he pointed down towards commercial fishing vessels near the small sand bars that clustered together in the channel. John thought for a moment that he saw the captain of one vessel wave, but it could not have been possible because of the distance.

To the drivers of other cars, they would seem nothing more than a happily married couple on a weekend trip, free from the monotony of work and the shared daily routine of suburban life – their greatest concern being not to get sunburnt.

John looked at James in the rearview mirror and spoke loudly, almost shouting, "I think that we three need a big ice cream. What do you think?"

"Yes, yes," said James with an equally loud voice. It was the first words John had heard him speak. Before James had only communicated by pointing or by shaking his head. Frowns and smiles had vividly communicated his feelings.

"Karen, I think James just passed his first hearing test," John said with a smile.

John pulled into a small ice cream shop. He opened the door and lifted James out of the car. Even though his fatigue had not left him, he felt a renewed energy. Perhaps it was the salty air that he breathed deeply into his chest as though it were an elixir. Perhaps it was when James put his arms around his neck that he felt most alive. For the first time since his illness, he realized that he might have a role to play in other people's lives.

Karen rounded the rear of the SUV and extended her arms to take James.

"No," said John. "This young pirate belongs to me. I have kidnapped him and shall now force him to reveal a great secret to me." Mimicking a figure of authority, he looked at James. "James, what flavor of ice cream would you like?"

"I want chocolate, Captain Pirate."

John glanced at the young teenagers who were staring at them. "My mate says he wants a scoop of chocolate ice cream. That is unless he wants two scoops."

"Two scoops, Captain," James said, loudly laughing.

Karen realized how deeply she missed having an adult companion. She knew how important this moment was to all of them even if it were only ice cream on a hot mid-summer morning. Inwardly she had expected the worst from John, thinking he probably only desired to be with her and being kind to her son was but a stepping stone to getting her into bed. She understood that James was as important to him as she was, if not more so.

Karen realized that John saw his own reflection of need in James. The need to belong, to hold and to be held. She realized he understood James in a way that no one else could, not even her. It was like two souls reaching out for each another.

John looked at him. "Sir James now wears a beard of chocolate. I thought pirates only had whiskers in their rum." James did not understand what whiskers were nor did he understand the meaning of rum. Regardless, he gave a large smile and licked the chocolate off his lips.

"Now my young lad, we need a vessel for you to command. What say you and the missus to a ride on the Port Bolivar ferry? A fine vessel she is indeed. If she is a stout ship, we will have to take command of her."

Karen laughed. "Sir Pirate, the brave captain just survived being a victim of chocolate on his shirt. What choice do mates have when he so commands?"

They drove down Broadway past the great mansions from the Victorian period. John had lived in Galveston when he was in elementary school and his father had lectured at the University of Texas Medical School located on the island of sand.

He had always envied the great wealth that gave rise to the Moody Mansion, the Bishop's Palace and the Sealy House. That was until today. To him they now represented the melancholy ruins of other people's lives. They were only temples dedicated to capitalism, empty rooms made of exotic wood. Stained-glass shadows hid while sunlight climbed the silent stairs.

"THERE SHE IS, YOUR COMMAND, CAPTAIN JAMES." Before them was the ferry that connected Galveston with Port Bolivar. John looked at Karen. "The 2.7 mile ferry ride offers a view of Seawolf Park and the Intercostal. It only takes eighteen minutes to cross one of the world's busiest waterways. It should really impress a seagoing fellow like young James."

As John carried James, they walked aboard. Proceeding toward the observation deck, they went outside to see the intercostal waterway and the ocean going vessels that transverse it. Soon they felt a surge of power as the ferry, filled with cars and trucks, left its mooring to sail across the narrow channel.

"James, if you look over there," he said, pointing, "you will see Pelican Island. There is an old World War II submarine moored in the sand. I think it is the USS *Seawolf*." John pointed once more towards Pelican Island. "My father said there was once an old quarantine station where that grove of oak trees is now located." John paused as they viewed a large partially submerged ship. "Look over there," he said as he pointed towards the ship. "You really blasted her out of the water. Well done, James."

Karen looked at John. "What in the world are you talking about?"

"Oh, I am sorry. Sort of got carried away there. It is all that remains of one of the few concrete ships ever built in the world."

"Are you kidding?" asked Karen in a serious tone.

John replied, "It's the truth. She is the SS *Selma*, an oil tanker, launched in 1919. It seems like the U.S. didn't have the steel to keep building new vessels so someone came up with the idea of building concrete ships. She is the largest one ever built. On a voyage early in her career, the SS *Selma* hit something in Mexico – a pier, I think. They scuttled her there just off Pelican Island after trying to patch her up without success. She is home to both sea birds and the imagination of young boys."

James had fallen asleep in John's arms as he was explaining the history of the ship.

"Let's go inside and get out of the wind," said Karen.

Once they were inside the less noisy cabin, the purring of the engines and the groans of the ship created a white noise that produced a sense of calm. John said, "Now you need to stop being the mystery woman and tell me about yourself."

"There is not much to tell. I have led the pretty typical life of a schoolteacher. Before I married Mark, I attended the local community college and later transferred to Texas A&M in Commerce, Texas where I graduated with a degree in education. I cannot believe you and I are both Aggies. A few graduate courses later, I was certified as a media specialist, you know, a librarian. Mark was a coach at the school where I worked. He was good-looking and very athletic. I thought he possessed all the qualities of a great husband and father. He not only coached but taught history as well. Later he resigned and started selling insurance. Mark wanted to make more money even though our salaries were enough for a small family just starting out in life. Being outgoing, he was perfect as a salesman and before long he had his own agency. In the meantime, I found out I was pregnant with James."

Karen observed the sea through the large window. "Everything was well at first. Getting pregnant was the best thing that had ever happened to me. Mark didn't seem to be bothered by the fact that I was pregnant, but neither was he excited about it. I can't even count the number of barbecues we were invited to. He would load up the pickup with his BBQ pit and Lone Star beer. If Mark was there, everyone knew it was going to be a great party."

Karen paused. "I began to realize that his love was for other people and for his job. The ob-gyn told me how well the pregnancy was going. Before long I was the proud mother of a seven-pound, three-ounce little boy. He was so cute, so handsome. Later on, people complimented James for his beautiful, curly blond hair, just a perfect baby. He had just learned to walk when he started showing signs of the tumor.

"At first, I couldn't believe it. I just sat there in my doctor's office arguing with him that he must be mistaken. 'There is absolute nothing wrong with my beautiful James!' I would shout amid tears. My husband never took us to see the doctor. He was always coaching or going to an out-of-town game. Can you imagine a father being so indifferent to his son? It hurts to talk about it even now, but I realize that you need to know more about us."

After breathing deeply, Karen continued, "Mark wanted nothing to do with imperfection. He looked at himself as being perfect both physically and professionally. What a delusional fool. After he left us, I went home to my mom. The place a woman always goes to when tragedy hits. After nights of crying to my mother, I returned to work.

"Yet I found it almost impossible to continue my job as before. Teachers quickly began to ignore my somewhat erratic behavior. They would walk into the teacher's lounge and find me crying. Have you ever noticed how people want to avoid you when you need them most?

"Eventually I resigned and returned home again, hoping my mother would be able to take care of us financially. What made it so sad for Mom and me was that my own father had left both of us when I was very young. Have you ever noticed how separated parents create divorced children?"

She paused as though the view of the sea could provide answers. "I knew that no matter what happened to us, I would keep looking for that magical cure for James. He is the only important thing in my life. My days begin with my feeding him and end with his bath. Now my time is also spent waiting for James to complete his treatments. See, I told you my life was not very interesting."

Unlike with Edna in Boston, he listened intently to every word she said. John noticed that Karen was beginning to cry. He reached over and took James from her arms. He held him very tight, then hugged Karen. It was as though walls were crumbling within him. John could not understand what was taking place within his own heart. He knew there was no way he could love someone so quickly. She and James were only strangers. Why this outpouring of emotions for two people that he would have to leave soon? He remembered the words of Shakespeare's "Sonnet 73":

This thou perceivest, which makes thy love more strong,
To love that well which thou must leave ere long.

He had memorized a few verses of Shakespeare but had quickly forgotten most of them. However, these words never left him. He was now keenly aware of the brevity of life and how each moment was precious – a gift.

John watched the sea from the window as Karen had done. The wind was blowing strong producing small whitecaps on the waters of the Intracoastal Waterway. Large ships crossed their course as the ferry continued its journey, ships destined for the ports of the world: Hong Kong, Tokyo, and Cebu. For a moment, he longed to be back at sea, free from the problems of the land and even free from James and Karen. Then he realized that he could not be free from himself. He remembered when his ship assisted another vessel in distress, how the shipwrecked sailors swam towards anything that promised to keep them afloat. He knew he and Karen were both doing the same thing.

CHAPTER 3

An Island Interlude

"LET'S EAT AT PIER 24 JUST OFF THE STRAND," John said to Karen in a quiet voice so as not to awaken James. "It is a place where James can see the seagulls and the small boats in the harbor. I read about the restaurant on the Internet. I am very hungry. What about you and James?"

Karen glanced at John. "That sounds wonderful. I must warn you that James doesn't eat much solid food. They have given him a port for his feeding tube. I think he will enjoy tasting the food, but I fear he won't be able to ingest much of it no matter how good it is. Just remember that when ordering."

They walked to their car with John still holding James. His small body sweated profusely in the warm sunlit air. The drive to Pier 24 did not take long. John parked the SUV after letting James and Karen off at the dockside. Overhead, large cottony clouds rolled across the sky providing an infinite variety of shapes for children to enjoy.

As Karen waited for John, James pointed to a cloud and smiled. Karen could not make out an image but was happy that James could see something that pleased him. "Look there, look there, Mom! See, that's us!" Karen looked again but only saw the abstract shape of a large distant cloud that was in the process of forming a thunderhead, the large anvil reaching for the heavens.

"Oh, James, I see it too," she said with a smile.

In the distance were the tall masts and furled sails of the trading barque *Elissa*. Anyone who looked at her would immediately conjure up images of the past, a time when the sails of the barque captured the four winds and spray drenched her forecastle under a tropic sun.

John soon joined them. "Now where would you like to be seated, inside or out? As for my mate James and me, I think we would prefer sitting outside. That way James and I can ensure that pirates don't board *Elissa*. I would hate for him to lose his new command."

They quickly ordered drinks and whatever dish struck their fancy. The plates soon arrived steaming, drenched in the odors of the sea. Despite the DO NOT FEED THE GULLS sign, John tossed his own shrimp into the air after seeing that James really was not hungry. Almost immediately, James too tossed a shrimp high into the air just as John had done. When the seagulls swooped to capture the food, James laughed. Soon there was no more shrimp left on either John's or James' plate. Karen then threw her one remaining shrimp as high into the air as she could. A large seagull swooped down and grabbed it. The waiters smiled as the birds dipped and rose on the currents of the warm salty air.

At a nearby table, small elementary-school girls covered their mouths as they talked while staring directly at James. He could not understand why they were looking at him instead of the gulls. Soon they too were laughing as John pretended to steal shrimp from Karen's plate. She pretended to hit him with her cloth napkin. Never had an uneaten meal tasted better to John. The world was kind and all things were as God had planned.

John pushed back his chair and rubbed his stomach indicating his satisfaction with the food. "Now that we have finished our meal, let's take a stroll along the seawall. My dad told me that great sea rats used to live under the granite boulders, but I think he was just joking."

After a drive to the Gulf side of the island, they walked along the concrete seawall looking at the large waves and smelling the drying seaweed that had accumulated in large amounts against the granite rocks that lined the base of the seawall. The seawall had been built to protect the island after the tragic hurricane of 1900 had killed thousands of people. In the distance, ships steamed towards various ports of the world. As they walked, James looked for the legendary sea rats.

When James pointed towards the walkway that led down to the sand, John said, "I tell you what, crew, let's sit on the bench and guess what ports those ships are headed to."

"I know, I know!" said James enthusiastically. "But I will not tell."

"I am going to demote you from Captain to swabbie if you don't tell," John said with a laugh.

"Okay, Captain Pirate, they are going home just like we are."

A small tear ran down Karen's cheek at the words. She looked at John for she, unlike the captains of the distant ships, did not know where their homeport was going to be.

"Well I be, Captain, you are right. They are going home indeed. I tell you what, there is a pier further down the seawall called the Pleasure Pier. I bet there are all kinds of fun things to do there if you and your mom don't mind."

James shook his head in a positive fashion as Karen smiled at them both.

They walked up the ramp to the Pleasure Pier and found themselves in a world of amusements. John looked at James. "First of all, I think the crew needs cotton candy. What do you think, Captain?"

James replied with a smile as he looked at John and pretended to eat an imaginary cotton candy.

"Now there is a ride that looks fun. I bet you and I can mount one of those horses on the merry-go-round."

John lifted James to a saddle as he climbed on behind him, holding him secure as the ride started. Each time their horse passed Karen who had chosen not to ride, John looked into her eyes. Her smile followed them around and around. Underneath the pier, the breakers of a wild sea crashed against the concrete pilings.

John held James tight against him as though protecting a wound in his side, afraid to let him go. James sensed the love that flowed from John but did not understand.

John's family used to live in the historic district of Galveston when his father lectured for a year at the Galveston Medical School. His father had little time for John and his mother was always engaged in various social events. Society and professional obligations demanded their time. It was as if John were only of secondary importance, the way a house cat would have been. It was only now that John realized how empty his parents' lives were and how they missed the many opportunities to share the moments of his youth with him. Perhaps that was why he held James so tight.

After returning to the car, John said, "Are you and James ready to see the beach house where we will be spending the night? It is just a few hundred feet from where the breakers fall."

Karen looked at him, her face solemn. "John, you could not have been nicer to James and me than you have been. I will always cherish this day. I am afraid, however, that we have both excited and tired James more than his doctor would approve. I guess what I am saying is that we need to get back to Houston."

John could only say, "I understand." Despite all his efforts to sympathize with Karen's need to return to Houston, he felt as though he had been rejected by her. He felt deeply hurt, the rejection he had experienced as a child.

As they drove back to Houston, James slept in his car seat. Karen had chosen to ride in the back with him. At that very moment, John felt very alone. "Does she not trust me? Did I say something wrong? Did she simply use me to fill up her day? Perhaps her husband did not really leave her, but is waiting for them." He was ashamed of many of his thoughts and knew them not to be true.

They spoke little in the hour-and-a-half drive to Houston. A few honking cars disturbed John's thoughts. Occasionally, he would look into the rearview mirror. James continued to sleep as Karen looked out the window, her face covered in tears.

CHAPTER 4

Disillusionment

JOHN'S TREATMENT PLAN INCLUDED radiation and chemo-therapy. Since the regimen was so demanding, he was given five days off to allow his body to absorb the medical abuse it had been given. John decided to return to his parent's house in Boston.

The sky was cloudy as the Boeing 737 touched down at Logan International Airport in the heart of Boston. Even though this was his parents' home, he felt like a visitor to the city, a mere sightseer of historic sites and fine dining.

Phillip was waiting for him in the airport's pick-up zone. The chauffeur and keeper of his parents' estate immediately got out of the family's Mercedes sedan when he saw John approaching. "May I help you with your luggage, sir?" he shouted over the roar of the shuttle buses and taxis.

"No need, Phillip. I don't have much with me, only a carry-on."

"As you will, sir," replied Phillip as he closed the trunk of the car.

The traffic in Boston was heavy. Phillip swerved in and out of the crowded lanes on his way to the estate. John looked at the harbor and remembered how much he loved the family catboat when he was a teenager. While his father never took him to Boston Red Sox games, he did enjoy taking the family with him on Sunday afternoon sails. Perhaps that was the only good memory he had of his childhood.

Soon the Mercedes stopped at the main entryway of the house allowing time for the large metal gate to slowly open. Phillip opened John's door. No one came out to greet him.

"Are my parents home?" asked John.

"They were when I left, sir."

"Oh, I understand." John went in to check the silver tray in the library for messages. Growing up he got used to the notes, usually tasks for him to complete, that his parents left him before going out.

John picked up the note written in a beautiful script:

Dear Son,

We will be away from the house for several hours. Your father has a speaking engagement at General. Ask Phillip to order you something.

Your loving parents

John walked up the two flights of stairs to his bedroom in the back which now served as a guestroom when his parents entertained or had houseguests on the weekend. His family was known to keep a fine liquor cabinet. There always had one or two guests who got too drunk to drive after a social function. John was certain that the bedroom frequently came to good use.

Some of his trophies and certificates of accomplishment had been removed from the room. It had been sanitized and staged to accommodate strangers. The hand-carved racers that had won blue ribbons in the pinewood derbies of his childhood were missing as well as the high school photograph of him in his tux. His mother had not approved of his date. Having just finished the novel *Shogun,* he had decided to ask a Japanese girl to the prom. It did not matter to them that her parents were both professors at MIT.

As he lay in bed, he thought about Karen and James. In some ways he felt angry at his own lack of trust in her, but in other ways he was just very sad. The room seemed so empty. Even the songs of the birds outside the windows were muffled and distorted. The air was controlled, not fresh as he remembered the sea breezes of Galveston.

He thought about calling Karen to ask how James was doing, but he put the phone down and laid back once more on his great-grandfather's mahogany bed. His parents claimed that his grandfather was an industrialist, but history revealed that he made his fortune off liquor and prostitution during the period of prohibition. The only thing his grandfather had done correctly, thought John, was to invest his newly gained fortune in Texas oil shares. That he did very well.

John realized he was falling in love with Karen, which was not something a person of his social standing should do. She did not graduate from an Ivy League school nor was her family in society, yet he longed for her. Perhaps he ached most for James. A child so innocent fulfilling, if only for a moment, his need to have a son. As he thought about the ferry ride and the meal at Pier 24, he fell asleep.

Suddenly he felt his arm being shaken. "John, John, wake up," a female voice said. "Your father and I will be eating in thirty minutes. It would be nice if you would join us for a change."

In the haze of sleep, John murmured, "Karen? Is that you, Karen?"

"I'm your mother," she said. "I don't know who in the world Karen is. Is that a friend you made in Houston?"

John propped himself up on his elbow. "Forgive me. I must have been dreaming."

THE DINING ROOM COULD EASILY HAVE SEATED TWENTY OR MORE GUESTS. Each place on the unoccupied table had a silver placeholder intended to identify the person who was to be seated at that particular location. The napkin rings held fine linen. The candelabra had been lighted since his mother loved candlelight even if there were only the three of them present.

John knew to stand by his designated place until his mother was seated. His father, upon entering the room shook his hand, and with the wave of his palm, indicated that it was time for both he and John to be seated. Such was the rigid formality that John had grown up with and was expected to pass on to his heirs. There was no deviating from tradition.

Phillip and a housemaid had prepared a fine dinner of wild Atlantic salmon, new potatoes, and asparagus spears. Not too heavy, but delicious enough to satisfy all. His father poured his mother's wine, his own and then passed the bottle back to Phillip who then proceeded to offer John a glass.

John's father glanced at him. "Tell me, son, how are things in Houston?" He paused as he looked for condiments. "Please pass the salt. I don't know why we must have such a long table. Did you ever meet Dr. Felgar? You know, he can be very valuable to you. He can also be a real asshole, but just overlook that part of his personality."

"No, sir," John replied after some hesitation as he carefully placed his napkin on his lap. Nervously, he began to roll the napkin ring in his hand.

His mother looked at him as Phillip poured more white wine. "You said something about a Karen when I awakened you. Please tell me who that person is. Do we know her family?"

"No, I don't think either you or Father would know her," John said as he sipped his wine.

"Well, son, you obviously know her. Should we learn more about her?" asked his father.

"No, sir, I don't think so."

"Such an ambiguous answer bothers me," said his mother. "Does she come from a Christian family?"

"By that, Mother, do you mean if she is Roman Catholic?" asked John, ignoring the fish Phillip offered him.

"Yes, that is exactly what I mean," said his mother in a slightly raised voice.

"Well, since you demand an answer from me: she is Mormon."

"Damn it, son," said his father. "I hope you are not serious. There has never been a Mormon in our family – and there never will be! They are nothing but heathens and lawbreakers."

John answered his parents' challenge, "Can't we eat one meal together without a trial taking place? In case you have forgotten, I am dying. What difference does it make if she is Hindu or Catholic? My god, how could such a question ever have occurred to either one of you?"

"Well, she is not dying," responded his mother.

"What does that mean?" John said.

"Even with your present medical condition, you are still a good catch," she said.

"A good catch! What for, to bury?" replied John whose hands were now visibly shaking.

His father looked at John sternly. "You know damn well what your mother is saying. You stand to inherit a very sizable trust fund. A substantial fortune left to you by your grandfather." Pausing, his father looked out the window as though to adjust his thoughts.

John rose from the table. "I want to clarify something. You are right, she is not dying. Her son is." With that remark he slapped his napkin on the table and left the room. As he walked out into the large ornate hallway, no voices could be heard in the dining room. His parents remained in shock at his reply and abrupt departure.

He fell asleep once more on his bed only to be awakened by a phone call from his former girlfriend, Edna.

"John, your mother said that you are visiting. I just wanted to check in to see how you are doing. Your mother told me what a rough time you are having. Gosh, I understand. My mom had breast cancer several years ago...."

John laid the receiver on the bed near to his ear and pretended to be involved in her remarks. Not truly listening, he responded with "yah" to her pauses.

Towards the end of her conversation he asked, "When did my mother call you?"

"Oh, just a few minutes ago. She said you were lonely and asked me to touch base with you. You know, renew an old friendship."

John found it difficult to control his anger. He knew his mother was trying to direct his attentions towards a suitable relationship. A woman who could not care less for him as a man but who, like livestock, had good breeding.

John felt vengeful when he responded, "Say, Edna, let's have a date tonight. I hear that Antoine's has improved the quality of their food. Is Italian okay? Even though Phillip prepared a great meal here at the house, I just was not hungry at the time. Right now, I could eat my own weight in food."

John remembered how much Edna hated Italian food. She said it always upset her stomach. He remembered how sick she became after finishing a selection referred to as the "Tour of Italy."

"Oh." Instead of declining, she said, "That would be nice, John. What time will you pick me up?"

"Let's just meet there. You know how radiation to the brain affects a man. I don't want to take any chances with you in the car. I will see you there at eight." With that comment, he dropped the receiver onto its holder. Edna also hated driving at night, not to mention the difficulty of finding a parking place near the restaurant. He knew he could not get a reservation this late on a Friday night, which meant they would have to stand in line for a long time. It would give him the chance to leave her with the excuse that he was too tired to wait. But later as he lay in bed awaiting eight o'clock, his anger subsided and he regretted treating her so poorly. It was not that he disliked Edna, he was just angry with his parents.

JOHN ARRIVED AT ANTOINE'S THIRTY MINUTES LATE. To his surprise, there was no long line outside so he entered the candlelit restaurant located in the Italian district of Boston. From a distant booth, he saw Edna wave.

She rose and embraced him. In some ways, she felt good. He knew her family and had attended Boston College, his freshmen year, with Edna and her brother, Edward. "Well, Edna, it is good to see you again. I have to admit I was concerned when you stopped responding to my e-mails, but what the heck, I can get over such minor stuff."

Edna looked at him as though she were observing on object of curiosity, similar to a freshman being introduced to her first lamprey in a comparative anatomy class. Even after they were seated, Edna continued to stare at him.

"Tell me, how is Edward doing? I assume he is still the same old asshole he used to be." Even though his comment presented a conversation piece, she did not respond. Her staring bothered him. "Edna, I assure you I have no electrodes or IV tubing on me. In fact, I feel very much alive and do not intend to die during the meal."

"Excuse me, John. I am sorry. I have heard so much about what you are going through that I just didn't know how to react to seeing you. Seeing a cancer patient always makes me feel ill at ease. I never know what to say. It is really silly of me."

John was still bothered by her lack of concern for him. "Why didn't you write once it became general knowledge that I was very ill? Surely my mother must have told your family about me."

"You know, I really cannot give you an answer. It seems like my life has just sped up. A new career and the things that go with it. You already know I am a little bit selfish. I always want things to go my way. Never having been really sick, I just could not empathize with you being so ill. You were always so full of life, especially in high school." Edna paused. "Now that I can think more clearly about it, I just didn't want to ruminate on it."

"Right before I was diagnosed, Jason mentioned you had found someone you really liked," John said, attempting to understand her better.

"Well, you know Jason, always the class clown. I admit I was interested in meeting new people, but who isn't? You can't hold that against me, can you? While you were in the Navy, I bet you were dating other women – you know, a girl in every port."

"Edna, I thought we had something special between us. We shared many interests together. The main thing going for us was that our families liked each another. You know how my mother thinks: 'Whoever you marry must be Catholic.'"

"We are similar, you and I. Maybe we should have gotten engaged before you left for the Navy. I didn't want to rush things. We were so young," said Edna as she looked at a couple seated at a nearby table. The man was holding the woman's hand as he spoke softly to her.

"Well, that doesn't apply now, does it? Suddenly events have changed. It is like I have a new reality, a narrow window from which I can view my life."

"Oh, don't talk so sad. You know how modern medicine is. I read about magical cures all the time. You will beat this before you know it."

"Edna, your fault never lay in your lack of optimism. Perhaps that is where we differ. Unlike you, I have thrown my rose-tinted glasses away. I am a realist now. "

"What is that supposed to mean? At least you're not quoting Jean-Paul Sartre. Oh, I forgot, he was an existentialist. Well, Mr. Realist, why don't you order me a glass of wine?"

It was the custom at Antoine's for a waiter to approach a table only if invited to do so. John waved his hand towards the server who reacted immediately.

Upon arriving at the table, the waiter uttered in a very quiet voice, "Sir, what wine would you and the lady care to drink?" He spoke with an Italian accent meant to please the clientele. In addition, he wore a large key about his neck that indicated his superiority over the other waiters.

"Let's have a mystery at our table. You bring us a bottle of your best red wine without telling us the name of the vineyard. My friend here will attempt to guess it."

"As you and the lady desire." With those words he vanished into the semi-darkness of the wood-paneled restaurant whose main source of light were the candles on the tables.

He returned and poured her just enough to sniff the bouquet. "Hmm," Edna said. "This is a hefty red. It must be Sangiovese. It is the perfect wine for tomato-based sauces and spicy dishes. The grower might be Antonelli whose vineyard is in Umbria."

The wine waiter gasped. "Madam, I have never known such a connoisseur of wine."

Edna smiled at both the waiter and at John. John spoke after the waiter had left. "Edna, you are probably right about the wine but more than likely incorrect about the grower."

"Well, if that is so, why do you think he complimented me?"

"He didn't compliment you. He complimented your ego. Do you honestly think he would tell you that you are wrong?"

"John, you can be so condescending. Why did you force me into a contest with a waiter?"

"Edna, he was no ordinary waiter, but a sommelier, a wine expert. It just shows you that we all have our price, even the best of us." He looked into her eyes. "I have to admit I am somewhat suspicious of you. You call me at my mother's request only after finding out my current condition. Now why would an ambitious woman do such a thing?

"Edna, the story of my trust fund has always been a joke. You may know that I will not inherit the money and properties until I am thirty. My grandfather felt strongly that a man is foolish until he is older. He thought that if I had learned to do without it first, then I would be wiser later. Perhaps he was right after all. I really have never found out what my life should be about. The irony is that I will inherit the estate while my will is being read.

"My grandfather greatly respected the writers of the biblical text, especially Solomon. The elder Johnson was not a moral man, but he admired the brilliance of its authors. He considered the Bible as the greatest work of literature that exists in the English language. He was very fond of this quote from Proverbs: 'It is better to dwell in the wilderness, than with a contentious and an angry woman.' Perhaps with age, a man can better distinguish between greed, desire, and love."

Edna's face reddened. "Are you saying that you think I would date and perhaps even plot to marry you for your mythical trust fund?"

"Unlike the sommelier, I do not say words that are chosen to please."

Edna pushed herself back from the table. "John, you are a son of a bitch and have always been one! You would not know compassion or love if it hit you solid in the face. The only reason I am not slapping you now is that you would not understand why I was doing it. Whenever we are together, you drag both of us down to a level I am not comfortable with."

"Edna, wait. I apologize for my rudeness. I know you are not after my inheritance. At least I can appreciate that. Please sit down," John said as he pointed to the chair she had vacated.

"Okay, I will – for just a moment until we can clear everything up between us."

"Thanks. I am no longer hungry. If you agree, let's enjoy the wine. I will order you something later, if you so desire."

"To be honest, I am not hungry either," said Edna, studying him as though wondering about his intentions.

John leaned towards her as he poured the wine. "Our parents always expected us to marry. After all, as a child, you were my best friend. Later on, I must say that you made one hell of a date."

"That is very nice of you to say that. Crude but nice. I guess it would have been only natural that we marry, we had so much in common."

"Perhaps that is what drove us apart. We didn't want to repeat our parent's lives. To sit in silent rooms, one reading the newspaper and the other a book. To find out at the end that we really never shared what was important."

"Okay, John, in your metaphysical way, what is important?"

John hesitated. "That is a great question that you assume I have the answer to. Let me be presumptuous and respond: it is to love not one's self but another."

Edna looked at him and laughed, "Now you have gone scriptural on me. I see that this need runs deep in your family," she said sarcastically. "Who among us would not put ourselves first?"

"Perhaps you have a better answer to share," replied John.

Edna replied, "'Love' is only a word. It is used too often. We have to be realistic each day. It is something that can be said, and immediately a person can act in any way he or she chooses. Your definition is unobtainable, childlike in its idealism."

"You are wrong. I did not say I had or could obtain such a lofty goal, but I have seen it in another. A mother's love for her child in Houston vividly showed me that it is possible."

The more they talked, the more convinced John was that Edna had no concept about what he was talking about. He had seen the love that Karen showed James. A bond that crossed all lines. To love her son so much knowing what must lie ahead for them both.

As they left the restaurant, Edna said, "Well, John, not a perfect evening, but an interesting one. Do you want to come by my apartment and see if we can improve on our relationship?"

"No, not really. I hope we can remain good friends."

"We will remain friends. I am certain our parents will see to that," said Edna as he closed her door. She did not look at him as she drove away.

THAT EVENING, JOHN WENT IMMEDIATELY TO BED. His meeting with Edna had not gone as planned. Perhaps he was too upset with her and his parents to allow himself to relax enough to enjoy her presence. After all, they had always cared for one another. He had even thought about asking her to marry him when he left for San Diego on his first ship. John wondered about what could have happened had he asked her to join him in California. Would it have worked out if both of them had tried?

Then he thought of Karen and James. Once more he questioned why she would not spend the night with him at the beach. Surely she did not think he would force himself on her. After all, his desire for sex had been impacted by the fatigue generated by the treatments. He realized she could not have known that he also had a change of heart when it came to what he wanted in a relationship.

ON MONDAY EVENING HE BOARDED THE PLANE BACK TO HOUSTON. He sat next to the window and watched the city grow smaller as he ascended into the darkening sky while a gentle rain fell on Boston.

He knew he was irreversibly being altered by forces he could not control. A strong feeling of loneliness came upon him as he leaned back against the seat and waited for what must lie ahead.

CHAPTER 5

The Uninvited

THE CITY WAS ARRAYED IN LARGE THUNDERSTORMS. Lightning arched from cloud to cloud, a beautiful sight of uncontrolled energy. John thought of the power of the proton beam, controlled, deliberate and deadly to the tumor inside him. Tossed by a strong cross wind, the plane bounced on the runway as it landed.

As he strode up the ramp to the terminal, he could hear the rain pounding on the walkway cover. He walked back down to his SUV and threw his carry-on into the backseat. He did not hurry for no one awaited him. He connected his GPS, not so much to find the place where he lived, but to make him aware when he neared an exit. The automated woman's voice guided him through the increasingly familiar streets that led to the up-ramp of the expressway.

The traffic was not as heavy as he had expected on the loop. Still he had to cross multiple lanes to make his exit. Horns sounded as he accidentally cut a driver off. Some had commented that Houston was a city of anger – perhaps that was true.

When he arrived at his apartment, he was greeted by a musty smell in the air. The carpet, walls and furniture contributed to the synthetic odor. He walked out to his balcony to water the few flowers he had purchased to make the apartment more cheerful. In his absence, they had lost their blooms and only their fingerlike stems remained.

HE AROSE EARLY ON WEDNESDAY FOR HIS TREATMENT. He realized that both his and James' appointments were at the same time. He knew there would be an awkward moment when he saw Karen again. Perhaps they would speak or find it more comfortable to ignore one another.

He arrived at the Center and descended the stairs. Karen and James were not there. He picked up a magazine and sat by the fountain until he was called for his treatment session.

Before he arose from his chair, he glanced at the other parents and their children. The children all looked so young, small, and frail. The parents shared looks of concern with each another. One mother had shaved her head so that she and her daughter would look alike. To him, the mother was beautiful in a way that he had never thought of before. "There is beauty in love," he thought.

No matter where he looked, no child was alone. He was very aware of the love being shown, far beyond what Edna or any other healthy person could comprehend. He noticed how someone always stepped forward to care for another, and he was thankful for that.

When he emerged from the treatment center, he started up the stairs and noticed the red stroller leaning against a couch. He knew it must belong to James. He hesitated on the stairs, unsure whether to leave the complex or remain. Then, for reasons unknown to him, he continued up the stairs and left the building. The bright light reflecting off the cars and pavement as well as the sounds of heavy traffic were no longer reassuring to him.

That evening he sat in his room looking at the street below. Before he knew it, twilight had turned into darkness. The streetlights turned on and the apartment was very silent except for the footsteps of the occupant above him. Whoever it was, the unknown person paced back and forth throughout the night – obviously a very troubled individual.

The next morning he exercised and, upon returning from the fitness center, sat alone eating breakfast in the small dining area of his apartment. Outside he saw a young couple walking with their two children. At that moment, he felt alienated from everyone. He knew that the clock would soon indicate it was time once again for his treatment.

The women and the men who administered the radiation were more than nice to him. In some ways, he looked forward to seeing them each day. He felt that he was forming true friendships with people he had not previously known. Their compassion with patients was very evident.

As he exited the double doors, he saw Karen helping James into the stroller.

John walked over and sat down by them for a moment. "Can I help you?" he said with a smile.

"That would be nice," said Karen. James looked at him though still just barely conscious from his having been put into a deep sleep.

"Captain Pirate, it's you," James said faintly as John lowered him into the stroller.

"Wait a minute, mate. Why am I giving you such special treatment? With your mother's permission, I am going to haul you up the stairs in my arms. Of course, you are a big, heavy fellow so it is easier said than done."

Both Karen and James smiled at him. James felt very cold as he carried him up the stairs. John noticed how red James' head had become from the radiation. His soft, flawless skin was now being affected by the treatment.

After putting James into his car seat, John turned towards Karen. "I feel very awkward. Please tell me if you prefer not to see me again. I know how it is with strangers. They can sometimes get too attached too quickly to you."

"No, no. Please feel free to help James anytime you want. It seems like I am always needing help."

John waited for a more personal response, but it did not come. "I hope you both have a great afternoon and evening. If you ever get too bored, please give me a call."

"Thank you John, you have been very kind to both of us."

Instead of getting his usual sandwich and bowl of soup at the Sweet Pickle, John drove to the toy store. There he got a cart and began to fill it with toys. The more he put in, the greater was his desire to add more.

At the checkout counter, the clerk looked at him. "You must have a large family, or is it a special birthday?"

"You could say it is a special birthday. You might even say it is my own."

The clerk conveyed a puzzled expression. "Whatever you say."

That evening John looked forward to the next day. He wanted to surprise James with all of the gifts he had purchased. Not having ever been a father, he was not sure what he should have bought. Perhaps some of the toys were not age appropriate but then he reasoned, "He will grow into them." His eyes moistened at the thought.

The sun was already sitting behind the live oaks that lined the street, the moon visible from behind the leaves of the trees. He was happy in his anticipation of the next day. He needed to see James smile.

The phone rang loudly, rousing him from his thoughts. He reached for the receiver expecting it to be a call from Karen. "Hello," he said cheerfully.

"Hello, John. It is Edna."

"Oh, Edna, it is nice of you to call."

"John, I still feel badly about how it went between us in Boston."

"That's okay. Nothing will interfere with our friendship."

"Would you like me to visit you in Houston? I understand that they have a lot of cultural events. I can always learn something there. Perhaps I could learn more about you than I know now, we have a lot of catching up to do." Uninterrupted by John, Edna continued, "You know what I would really like to do? Tour the missions in San Antonia and also visit Austin. My cousin, Margaret – you remember her – well, she wants to attend the University of Texas. By visiting the campus, I can give her my own impression. Her family really wants her to attend an Ivy League school, but she is young and headstrong. She heard that Texas is a party school, and with the music industry being located there, who at her age wouldn't want to be in Austin? She has time to learn from her mistakes."

John had not expected Edna to pursue him in Houston. He wanted to be free of her, that was true, yet he longed for companionship. Someone to talk to, perhaps even to wait for him while he underwent his treatments. "What have I to lose?" he reasoned. "Karen and I can just be friends, besides I can't see it going anywhere with her. Do I really want to be involved with Karen and James when I find it so difficult to handle my own problems?"

"Well, Edna, I am pretty busy in Houston. I am involved in a clinical trial related to radiation-induced fatigue. They have me exercising, taking pills and undergoing counseling sessions. I don't know if I will have the time for us to do anything should you visit me."

"John, are you telling me in a polite way that you would rather I don't come? If so, just say so. You have been always so truthful until now."

"Karen, how in the world can I judge my physical condition should you visit me out here? Some days I feel great. Other days I feel like shit. Do you really want to see me walking a treadmill when all I really want to do is sleep?"

"So, it's not a yes or no, but a maybe," she said sarcastically.

"At least you know the truth," replied John. Before he could say more, she had hung up. "Surely she got the hint! I really hope so," he thought out loud.

TWO DAYS LATER, HE HEARD A KNOCKING AT HIS DOOR. "Who in the world can that be?" he wondered. "I don't know anyone living in Houston and no one knows my address."

He walked slowly to the door expecting to see either a salesman or a Mormon. As he unlocked the door, he felt pressure against it and Edna stepped into his apartment and private world.

"Hello," he said reluctantly. "Edna, what on earth are you doing here? You should have called first."

"Why should I have called? You might have said no. This way you have to say yes to my being here."

"How in the world did you find me? Houston has over two million people living within its hinterland."

"You forgot something: your mom."

Unintentionally, John replied out loud, "Shit! I forgot about her!"

In Edna's hand was her one piece of luggage. A purse and laptop dangled from her shoulder. "Aren't you going to be a gentleman and help me?"

John did not know what to say. The last thing he wanted was to entertain someone regardless of who it was. Still he could not refuse such an obvious and demanding request. Yet the moment he touched her suitcase, he knew he was committed to her staying with him.

He took the suitcase from her hand. "Where will you be staying? As you can see, I have a one-bedroom apartment. Unfortunately, the sofa does not make into a bed."

She stared at him as though waiting for the punch line. "Why, we will share the bedroom, of course. You did mention that your treatments have reduced your sexual urges, which I remember were pretty strong. So, I think I will be very safe sleeping with you."

"Reduced, not eliminated." He could not help but smile when he spoke.

Whether she knew it or not, Edna created great anxiety in John. He had cherished his individuality in Houston, the freedom of opportunity, the diversity of selection whether it was in people or in food. He had always resented his mother's interference in his life, now Edna was determined to do the same.

"Okay, alright. I can't very well send you off. You need to know that I have treatments five days a week and I need to leave fairly early each morning. I hope I don't disturb you too much when I get up. By the way, how long do you plan on staying?"

She smiled at him. "Until the issues between us have been resolved."

"In other words, forever." He laughed. "Tomorrow is Friday. Would you like to spend the weekend in Austin or San Antonia?" He felt towards her as he would towards a cousin – it was his family obligation to entertain her. Inwardly, he welcomed her voice in his silent world.

After seating herself on the couch, Karen looked up at him. "You didn't mention Galveston. Isn't that city just a short distance from Houston? All of my friends who have been there really hated it, but I would like to see if what they say about it is true. It surely is not as dirty as they claim it to be."

The mere reference to Galveston put him on the defensive. He wanted to tell her that she did not deserve to visit the city, a place that he had shared with Karen and James. John did not want his memories of the island to be defiled by her.

He looked sternly at Edna. "Why would you want to visit a place that you think so little of?"

"John, your memory must have been affected by your treatments. Don't you remember that in law school I mentioned my interest in environmental law? If it is as bad as my friends say it is, I may consider practicing law there. With all the industrial pollution being emptied into the bay and its lax environmental standards, it should be very entertaining."

Edna did not sense how much John loved the island. The thought of someone like her wanting to dissect it bothered him.

Galveston to John was as much a dream as a reality. The thought that someone would go there to earn money filing lawsuits angered him.

"Edna, I have been to Galveston enough. I think San Antonio would be best."

"Well, I am not resting my case yet. We should have several weekends to look the area over."

John did not know how to react. She continued to outmaneuver him at every turn. Other than his trust fund, why would she be so interested in him? She was hardly the type to wait on the sick.

In some ways, he was attracted to her. The long black hair that she wore up invited him to loosen it. Her figure, accented by tight clothing, showed that she had a great interest in attracting men. It was obvious that she worked out at some health club in the city. There was an ongoing fitness mania in Boston. Every yuppie was a member of a club, a place where people sweated together but did not speak.

Her clothing fit her social status. Judging from her Louis Vuitton luggage, she had an outfit for every occasion whether it was formal dining or tennis. Her makeup appeared professionally applied like that of a celebrity hosting a game show.

She was apparently a very artificial person, a product of her own personal belief that perfection could be obtained and that the inhabitants of the earth, by birth alone, were weaker than she was. She felt that John existed solely for her and that she would own him regardless of cost.

With her good looks and family money, she could have whatever she wanted. Earlier she had rejected John since he was too easy. Now that he appeared to be a challenge to her, he was interesting. Besides what did she have to lose? His mother had told her mother that John was terminally ill. She loved the fact that she had only so much time in which to beat him, a perfect challenge to her canine instinct.

When John returned from the bedroom where he placed her luggage on the luggage rack, she expected him to embrace her. Instead he walked into the kitchen and drank a glass of water in front of the sink.

Karen smiled at him. "My, my, water? What happened to that young man who could go through a six-pack before lunch? I hope you have something stronger than that for me?"

"No, afraid not. I can't drink any alcohol while undergoing treatment."

"What a bore! I guess I will have to drink alone?"

"Yes, if you are going to drink at all."

"You are a man and, based on that fact, you have weaknesses. I can guarantee you that you will be drinking by the time I am done with you."

"Shall I be reading Judges 16 in preparation for this challenge?" From his childhood readings of a Bible left by the Gideon's, he remembered both the strength and weakness of Samson.

"Are you to be guided by a fantasy?" she said, laughing.

As the colors of the sky changed hues, they left for a nearby steak house. John could eat meat and potatoes, but not salads or raw vegetables. He was tired of the monotony of his diet. He longed for just a hamburger and Coke. He no longer cared about the name of the restaurant or who might be there. When it came to evening attire, he preferred old, worn cargo pants and a pullover. Edna, however, did not tolerate the clothing of people she referred to as "common." When she dressed, she dressed for success.

They arrived at Carafate's just as its yuppie clientele arrived. The line was long and the lobby only had a few seats for those waiting to be seated. John gave his name to the hostess and went to lean against the outside wall where others had congregated to smoke. Several of the clientele were smoking profusely. His lungs, still sensitive from a recent bout of bronchitis, felt irritated.

"Why are you leaning against that dirty wall? You have an expensive sports coat on. What would your mother and father think of you?" she said with a smile while her real intention was to correct his newly acquired sloppy habits. "Just think of how sweet I am being to you. If you haven't even noticed, I quit smoking."

"A wise decision. I used to smoke, too. More than I should have, but I had to quit. I know it will not last. Bad habits always return," said John loudly over the piped-in music flooding the waiting area.

"Yes, your mother told me you have stopped. I couldn't be outdone by you. If you can do it, so can I." To Edna, everything was competition. The inborn need to outdo another. She loved both the hunt and the kill.

"Well, John, since I have you up against the wall, where are we going this weekend?"

"I think that San Antonio would be a great place. The River Walk is nice as well as the missions that stretch from the city south into a unique part of Texas. Who knows, you might find the San Antonio River polluted."

"John, that's not fair. Just remember that we will eventually need to go to Austin. Margaret will kill me if we don't."

"Sorry, I do hope we get served before the street cleaners arrive. I should have gotten a reservation." John felt very weak for he had not eaten since the peanut butter on toast he had early that morning. He was beginning to feel cold and clammy too, but did not want to tell her. He never wanted to admit a weakness to Edna.

As he looked at her standing so straight in her perfect skirt, he wondered why he had not told her to go to hell. Perhaps it was the loneliness within him. He had never felt that way before meeting Karen and James. To him, they were the opposite of Edna, yet he felt rejected by Karen. He felt that his life was already filled with enough anxieties to add any more. In the last few days, he had sought peace but could not find it. John had never found the green pasture and the quiet stream that ran through it that David had spoken of. He then remembered his favorite quote from Jean Paul Sartre: "Hell is other people."

"Johnson – party of two!" sounded from the speaker system. He followed Edna into the deliberately darkened interior of the restaurant. On the tables were battery-operated candles whose synthetic flames moved to a preprogramed pulsating rhythm.

Edna dutifully waited for him to pull back her chair. Once seated, she asked, "What shall we talk about?"

John hated the impersonal "we." He preferred the stronger "I" and "you." Besides he knew she was going to dominate the conversation. His task, he realized, was to keep his mind from wondering too far off from the conversation that Edna planned to have with him.

After marshaling his courage, John blurted out, "Edna, I don't have a planned agenda. I would rather have a free-flowing evening."

"Not I," she replied. "I like figuring out mazes. They are so much more interesting. Let's start with your naval career."

"Are you kidding?" he replied. "Who wants to talk about military shit? Let me guess, you're from Fox News."

"Touché. Never mind. Well, uh, tell me about your girlfriends. Growing up, didn't you have something going on with Nattie? I always thought she was a slut. You can correct me if you like."

"Just because someone liked me in high school, you assume she was a slut. The most we ever did was kiss. You forget how young we all were then. We still had none of the bullshit that comes with growing up."

"Well, you may have been boring back then, but I had lots of boyfriends, and we did everything."

"What do you mean by 'everything'?"

"Promise you won't tell your mother."

"That is one thing you can be certain of. She is the last person I would tell anything to. No, wrong, the last person I would tell anything personal to would be my father."

"Well, besides drinking too much, we did the party scene when it came to drugs. You know, all the popular ones. Lord, I am just thankful I stopped short of heroin. I understand that you get hooked with just one dose," said Edna confidentially.

"Drugs weren't my thing. A beer or two and that was it. There is too much in life to do than to get stranded on a lee shore by street drugs."

Edna smiled. "I never realized how boring you really are. Tell me, at what age were you deflowered?"

"You know, I am not really comfortable talking about me."

"I lost my virginity when I was fourteen," Edna admitted proudly. "Can you believe it? I really didn't know what it was about. Some exchange student from Germany was staying in our guesthouse. He was so cute. Blonde hair and blue eyes, you know, all that stuff."

John said confidently, "Well, I will tell you this much – you have me beat on that score. I was certainly older than fourteen."

"I know guys don't mature as quickly as girls do. I can't figure why that is. Then once they mature, all they think about is sex," said Edna, amused by the conversation.

"Really? Who is conducting the discussion now?" questioned John.

"Well, I have a right to know more about you. I have to admit I was a little jealous of Nattie even if your affair occurred in high school and was only from the neck up. Why you went with her I will never know. She wasn't from a good family. Besides, she was underdeveloped for her age. No boobs at all. Just a stick with a bush of black hair on the end."

"Edna, tell me, what does constitute a 'good' family?" inquired John. "I am really curious."

"Good question. You always did pose interesting ones. To me a good family has a traceable history. You shouldn't have to use one of those genealogy websites to discover who you are. Can you image me using one of those DNA sites to see if I am really English? I consider that as degrading as trying to meet someone online. What a bunch of losers!"

John realized that he had hit one of Edna's hot buttons and immediately regretted it. Edna continued, almost shouting, "You should be able to open a book in a library and find your family's name mentioned prominently and frequently. Since accumulating wealth and position is an indicator of IQ, having money is an indicator of a successful bloodline." With her observation, she paused expecting him to challenge her comments.

"Edna, not to stray too much from your topic, but I want to talk a little bit more about our planned trip on Saturday. I am thinking we could start with the southernmost mission and work our way north. The southernmost one, Mission Espada is the smallest of the group, but the most interesting one for me, perhaps because of its compactness. You really get a feeling of how people lived in the early 1700s."

"My lord, how many churches – I mean, missions, are there?"

"Five if you count the Alamo."

"Oh my, you mean five churches to see in a Texas summer without air-conditioning? I bet you haven't been to that many churches in your life. Will it count as penance if I see all five?"

"No doubt such an experience would ensure that you go directly to heaven – thus skipping purgatory, which in your case is optional."

"Please tell me they are not just empty buildings with headsets as tour guides. I can't stand headsets."

"The missions are what you make them out to be."

Edna could not help but comment, "Well, the Irish certainly knew how to live. They have turned some of their protestant churches into nightclubs."

"Edna, I hate to detract you from your observations regarding faith, but we do need to order. After all, this is an Italian restaurant with a very good reputation for the quality and variety of its menu offerings."

Edna quickly scanned the menu. "I want you to know how brave I am for eating Italian. The last time I had that 'Taste of Italy' meal, I got deathly ill."

"Edna, aren't you exaggerating a little?"

"John, I will not described it in detail. Just use your imagination."

AFTER DINNER, JOHN RECEIVED THE CHECK FROM THE WAITER who seemed almost apologetic for charging him. Without looking at the cost, John inserted his credit card in the holder.

"Aren't you going to see how much you have been charged?" Edna asked in a serious tone.

"I will figure the percentage of the tip when he comes back."

"You must get cheated a lot. I always look at the bill before paying it. Of course, you do get a reprieve before you sign."

"Edna, I imagine that you examine everything before agreeing to it. In a way, it sums you up. You have always assumed that people are going to cheat you or cheat on you."

"Well, was I wrong?" asked Edna. "I know I left you, but it really didn't matter. You and Sarah were an item, and I knew it. You virtually screwed her with your eyes in front of me."

"Sorry, but who's Sarah?" asked John.

"Don't act like an innocent freshman fraternity member. You know damn well I am talking about Sarah Miles."

"You have got to be kidding! I could certainly have done better than Sarah. She was only a nice person who happened to be a friend."

"I am sure you tried to have sex with her."

"I am flattered that you think I can get dates that easily."

"Okay, John, let me tell you something: Sarah was only after your money. She knew what you were worth or at least she thought so. With your mother in the society pages each goddamn day, the whole world must have known that anyone in your family would have been a good catch, even your father." She continued, "The rumor was that you got clap from her – that was why I quit dating you, you sorry son of a bitch!"

"Edna, calm down. That was years ago. Sarah is not the piranha you think she is. Anyway, I managed to get out of her life without losing any flesh. That wasn't necessarily true when we were dating." John looked more closely at Edna whose features appeared very sharp in the light of the artificial candle. "Let's get real and look at today. I am not anyone's idea of a man that a woman would want to be with. It is sapping the strength I didn't know I had just to be here with you tonight."

"I am sorry, John. Really I am. Will you overlook my thoughtlessness for once? I know I exaggerate things for effect. It is just my nature." She paused. "John, I realize I have been doing it too often. It is a bad habit for a lawyer to have."

"You certainly have a way of expressing your feelings in a blunt manner, and I admit it makes me very nervous," John said, touched by her rare display of self-awareness. Deep down, he wondered whether finding a weakness, any weakness, in others was what attracted him to them.

CHAPTER 6

An Unexpected Detour

Upon RETURNING TO HIS APARTMENT, John felt very awkward as he opened the aluminum door with its two deadbolts. He was still at a loss regarding their sleeping arrangements. His back would not allow him to sleep on the couch. Perhaps he could sleep on the floor, but that too would be painful.

When they were young, she had been the aggressor. He had always submitted to her strength. In college, she was as enthusiastic in making love in a motel swimming pool as in the family car.

Edna was not the type of person who cared about what others thought. John was the exact opposite. She was fun and, as she would often tell her friends, he was boring.

If anyone had ever seen them having sex in a motel pool, no one had reported them. It was just easier that way since calling the police would mean appearing in court as a witness. Watching them was probably more entertaining than what any motel guest would see on the television.

But things were different now. He knew that she had not changed from the rude, sarcastic, sexually enticing woman he had known in college. The girl that would risk anything for fun. He was the one who had changed. He now sought moments of quietude, content to listen to classical music and be alone. To him a perfect day was spent on his sailboat, feeling her sea-induced motion and watching the seagulls overhead drenched in the warm sun. He no longer dreamed of sailing his vessel to the Pitons or around the Cape of Good Hope. He now sought simpler, purer things. Perhaps he was becoming more spiritual, yet he worshipped no god.

One of his favorite quotes came from the Romantic poet, John Keats:

> *Give me books, fruit, French wine and fine weather and a little music out of doors, played by someone I do not know…*

"Edna, you may find it strange, but I do not want to make love tonight. I will sleep with you, but nothing more."

"Are you, John Johnson, afraid of getting aroused? Am I with the wrong man? I remember when we screwed on top of the library one night. I am sure the people walking below us wondered what on earth was going on three floors up. You couldn't get enough of me then. I see that I am going to have to work on you," she said, smiling in a mischievous manner. She stepped into the bedroom and opened her valise. From it she produced a pair of panties that she held up in front of John. "In case you are wondering, I do occasionally wear pajamas."

John sat in the living room for a long time. He stepped out onto the balcony and lit a cigarette, one that he had saved for a "just in case" moment.

Then she emerged from the bedroom dressed in her panties and nothing more.

"Edna, I am afraid you will have to wear something more. Look in the dresser and get one of my pajama tops. It is a requirement that comes with my bed."

"Good grief, a prude and a lover of Spanish missions. How can a girl compete with that?"

"You will someday learn that life is not all about trust funds and sex. There is more to it. There has got to be."

"Well, if you don't want me tonight, you will later. You keep dwelling on your illness. You look just fine to me. I think you are hiding behind it as an excuse not to take part in the real world. The same thing that you accused me of earlier."

"Okay, I am not perfect, I am just simply changing. Trying to evolve into something that is better than I used to be."

Edna flashed him the look of an inquisitor and entered the bedroom, knowing he would shortly follow. John put on his pajamas in the bathroom and, rather than getting into bed with her, walked once more onto the balcony of his apartment. He lit another cigarette and looked at the moon as it rose above the live oaks. The warm summer air had the pungent odor of leaves. An evening dove called and he was alone. After closing the French doors, he sat on the couch and immediately fell asleep.

The next morning, he made coffee and waited for Edna to emerge from the bedroom.

"My god, what time is it?" she said. "The sun woke me up through the cheap blinds. From the sound of traffic outside, I assume no one sleeps late in Texas. Mr. Trustfund, couldn't you have afforded a better apartment than this?"

"I have made some coffee. It is time we get dressed and get started. I know you don't usually get up until afternoon, but we have a trip before us."

"Oh Lord, don't remind me of that. Can't we trade out? Let's go to Lake Travis near Austin in exchange for your not having made love to me."

"What on earth? Why would you want to go to one of the highland lakes?"

"Well, you like boats," she replied. "They might even have a sailboat for us to rent. I looked it up on my laptop before I fell asleep last night. There wasn't anything else to do since you never came to bed. Lake Travis is supposed to offer good sailing and clean, clear water due to the limestone. Do you mind? I don't think I can take on empty missions and taped tour guides."

"THANK GOD FOR GPS," JOHN SAID as he traversed the highways and rural roads that led them from Houston to the lake. The wild odors of Texas entered the vents of the SUV, the earthy scents of cedar and live oak. As he drove, he looked at the myriad colors of Indian paintbrushes and wild bluebonnets that lined the roads and grew abundantly in the distant meadows.

John had bypassed Austin and taken the Round Rock exit to the lake. He was anxious to avoid Austin with its traffic congestion. More than that, he was anxious to be on the water even if it was with Edna. She seemed to have changed on the drive, being quieter than usual and less aggressive than she usually was. Perhaps his physical rejection of her the night before had stung her deeply.

It then occurred to John that she was simply in the process of changing tactics. She was beautiful and deep down he did want to have sex with her. In some ways, he regretted not having gone into the bedroom and embraced her as she had expected. He began to wonder what he was trying to accomplish with his prudish attitude.

He did not love her and could have at least used her. But he would have gotten too close to the flame, which was probably her intent.

From the bluff above the lake, they saw the flat-topped hills of Texas. Hills that appeared to have been mountains until some giant had taken a tomahawk and cut their tops off. Such was Edwards Plateau with its prickly cactus, yucca, cedar and live oak. It stretched before them until it reached the clear, blue western sky. Down below, Lake Travis appeared as a great blue dragon resting in a limestone den. Upon the surface, myriad sails could be seen as a small regatta beat to windward.

From there they traveled to a marina that rented small sailboats by the day or weekend. Plastic shells with a mast and two sails, the synthetic main and jib. John thought about how alive his own sailboat was with its smell of hemp and canvas compared to these indestructible glass-hulled boats. Even the wooden catboat owned by his father was like a living thing – it could be easily damaged by his own hand at the tiller or by that of another.

Edna was wearing a sky-blue tank top and tan shorts underneath which she wore a white bathing suit. In a moment they were on the water beating to windward. The spray from the waves drenched them in clear, almost drinkable water that cooled their sun-warmed skin. The wind was unusually strong. They had to lean out on the rail in order to keep the boat from capsizing, their hearts racing as they rode the wind of a fresh southeast gale, their hair tossing about like telltales.

When an unexpected gust of wind came at them, they found themselves suddenly thrown into the warm water. Emerging, they laughed together as they used to in college. In all of their sailing together on both the saltwater bays of New England and the large swells of the open Atlantic, they had never capsized before.

Thanks to its fixed keel, the day sailer immediately righted itself without them aboard. The anchor, however, had fallen overboard when they had capsized, mooring the boat to the shallow bottom.

"Well, Captain Trustfund, you seem to have stranded us in paradise," Edna said jokingly. "Let's remove our clothes and inspect the hull for damage."

In a brief moment, they both were naked. The sun was bright as they stroked the water, splashing one another and laughing. All of a sudden, John felt alive, free of inhibitions, and very thankful for the moment.

"Captain Trustfund, do you have any beer aboard?" she asked.

"Well, Ms. Edna, I sure do. I will go get it. When I return with a beer or two, would you mind dropping the trust fund joke?"

"Now that I have you naked, I will do what I want. Men have the most difficult time saying no when they are without clothing," she said with a smile. "Getting beer is a job for a mate, not a captain." With that, she hoisted herself on the sea ladder hanging over the stern of the boat. He could not help but admire her perfectly tan body as she lifted her legs over the rail. "Where's the beer?" she asked.

"It's in a white cooler," shouted John as he continued to tread water.

"There is no white cooler here," she shouted back.

John peered into the water. "Oh no! We will have to dive for it. It is sitting on the edge of a rock shelf about ten or so feet down."

Instantly Edna did a perfect swan dive off the boat, her body slicing through water without any spray. In less than a minute, she returned to the surface holding two Lone Star beers in her hand. They then found a boat seat that had formerly served as a life preserver. For a short period of time, they floated, mesmerized by the warmth of the sun and the gentle rocking of the cushion.

Soon they were holding on with one hand and sipping a beer with the other as they looked into each other's eyes. Resistance quickly passed from John. Her body was all that he desired. His philosophy about life and its ultimate meaning was lost in a moment.

They tossed their beer cans as they embraced. Like diving seabirds, they made love while descending in the clear water of the warm lake.

As THE SUN TURNED A PLUM COLOR, the wind softened as they sailed under the myriad stars of the clear Texas night sky. Quietly the hull moved as the moon once more arose over the hills that guarded the lake. They could not feel any wind, yet the small vessel continued to maintain its meandering course. A course that followed the stars, each one representing a new heading as they voyaged among the constellations.

They made love once more as the calm ushered in a night breeze that was strengthened by the force of a distant thunderhead. A curtain of clouds descended upon the stars as thunder shook the valley through which the lake flowed.

Upon the rising wind, they sailed to the marina.

DRIVING BACK TO HOUSTON, John did not know how to interpret his feelings toward Edna. She had won as she always did. Even though he was not married, he felt as though he had betrayed someone, perhaps himself.

After he and Edna had showered together in the apartment, he expected to make love once more to her.

Edna interrupted his intentions, saying, "John, I know this is not what you expected, but I am ready to go back to Boston."

"But why? I thought you had a great time on Lake Travis. We were finally communicating with each other."

"I know. You are too nice a person for me. While I can fake a relationship, you and I will never make it as a couple. Your suspicions were correct. I was interested in your money. You see, Dad lost a great deal in commodity trading, something to do with copper. I was trying to secure my future by manipulating you. In the end, I just cannot go through with it. You had me figured out at the very beginning."

"It is not like you to quit. Is it because of my illness?"

"Yes, it is. I don't want to love you only to lose you. I know it is strange and probably very selfish. I am so sorry."

CHAPTER 7

An Interlude

THE FOLLOWING DAY, JOHN TOOK EDNA to Hobby International Airport. Before she went through security, they embraced.

"You know, John, you are worth loving," she said. Tears ran down her cheeks, distorting her eye shadow. He kissed her cheek tenderly, then she turned and vanished down an aisle filled with boarding passengers.

John felt very weak as though his energy had flowed into her. All about him, strangers embraced and departed. The bench he sat upon felt hard and cold as he waited for her plane to depart. He kept thinking that she would change her mind, but inwardly he knew that she would not. In the end, he had begun to love her. He too knew their love would soon end regardless of what they did. The cancer was growing, and he knew it.

MONDAY MORNING, HE ARRIVED BACK AT THE CLINIC EARLIER THAN USUAL. In some ways he felt foolish being there two hours ahead of time. The truth was the only people he knew in Houston were the nurses, technicians, doctors, and other patients. He was impressed by the medical team's friendliness and willingness to embrace a stranger. The other patients offered their friendship as well. Among them were commodity traders, a retired Air Force sergeant major, a manufacturer of portable buildings, the CEO of a mining company, and others in various professions and trades – all different, yet now the same. They had become his family and friends. Without them, there was no one else to talk to. No one else to dream with.

After his therapy, he lingered to talk with the other patients awaiting their own treatment. He poured himself a fresh cup of strongly brewed coffee as he looked for a familiar face. Suddenly, the doors opened and Karen emerged carrying a sleeping James.

At first he felt very uncomfortable. He looked at her, then looked away. Instead of walking out, she approached him. "Good morning, John. How have you been? It's been a while since we last spoke. I was afraid you were mad at me." As she waited for his reply, James stirred within her arms.

"Oh, just fine. Trying not to get rained on. Did you notice how bad the storm was last night? Thunder woke me at three this morning. I couldn't get back to sleep after that," he said, avoiding her eyes.

"We got a little wet coming into the building. I think James likes the rain. He never complained."

"Kids must be really adaptable. More so than adults," John said, looking directly at her for the first time.

Karen met his gaze as she rocked James back and forth in her arms. "I was a little surprised when you didn't call. James seemed to be waiting for someone. He kept walking or crawling to the front door and would just sit there. It broke my heart to see him so. He has never done anything like this even when his father was around. We both stayed clear of the doorway whenever his father arrived. Mark would come in, change his clothes, and cut on the news without noticing us. When the news was on, which it was for most of the evening, no one was allowed to talk. On weekends, Mark would go to some local sporting event. Of course, even before James' illness, he never took his son with him." She paused. "I think James was waiting for you."

"Karen, surely not. He doesn't even know me that well."

"I think he does. Kids can sense a person's character better than adults."

"Well, if I have to be well-thought-of by another, I am glad it is James."

James awoke in Karen's arms and stared at John as though attempting to recall the identity of a person he both trusted and cared for. He put his arms out to John who immediately took him from Karen.

"You know something, Karen, I have been really wanting a hamburger. One of those really big ones, you know, supersized, with lots of onions, tomatoes and lettuce. Of course, it has to be topped off with French fries and a large Coke. Do you think you and James would be interested in a lunch date? We can get James just about anything he wants. After all, it is almost noon."

Karen looked at John, then at James. "Of course, we will. I don't think we are going to get a better offer this morning. Do you still have that car seat in your automobile? I can't believe you bought one for our trip to Galveston."

"Yes, it is still attached to the backseat. Even a bachelor knows about the laws on child safety. It's not a big deal. The only problem I had was installing it. I must not be as smart as I thought I was. I ended up going to the fire station where they assisted me for free."

John buckled James into the car seat. He was still very sleepy as they left the Cancer Center. It was not long before John pulled into a Whataburger. As they entered the restaurant, he asked Karen what she and James would like to order.

When the food was delivered to their table, the smell was delicious to John. He allowed himself to relax. "Karen, I really did miss you. I feel like I am more complete in your presence. I never imagined I would miss you so much." He paused, sensing he had offended her. "That shows how foolish I am to stereotype my own thoughts. I have never known such a comfortable feeling as that of being with you." He looked at the child in her arms. "When I said 'you,' it included James."

"John, I know we are not all that easy to accept. As you know, I have made some mistakes in my life. We all eventually pay for our errors regardless of how small or trivial they may appear to be at the time, but I know one mistake that I did not make and that was having James. I don't think Mark really wanted a child, so you might say that my little boy was an accident, sort of like a miracle. Miracles are never planned, only asked for."

"Karen, I have to admit I was a little hurt when you refused to spend the night with me in Galveston. My intentions were pure, but you could not have known that."

"Would you have thought more of me had I accepted such an offer from a stranger?"

"You ask a question that is very difficult to answer. I think so highly of you that I would never question your past or the intent of your rejection."

"John, I didn't reject you. You are the only good thing that has come into our lives. Since I have to remain close to James at all times, I feared you would resent the fact that we have so little time together. Did you really think I didn't want to sleep with you? Rather than have sex, which I have done without since my husband left, I wanted to be held. I wanted your arms around me so that I could feel your strength. I feared that we both would have gone further than we had intended. I did not want you to regret it in the morning. See, James and I are a mess in the morning. His feeding tube needs to be cleaned, I have to prepare his formula, and he is always fussy when he wakes up. As for me, my hair is horrible and I would be without makeup. I can't take the time to look good when there is so much to do for him. I didn't want you to be disillusioned at the beginning of our relationship regardless of how short it may turn out to be."

John smiled. "I understand what you are saying. There are times with my own illness when I don't feel like getting out of bed. Yes, even now I am taking medicine for the nausea that never seems to leave me. It began when I needed to have chemotherapy in addition to my radiation. If there is anyone that knows what the morning can be like, it is me."

They sat there eating their hamburgers just as any American couple would on a Friday afternoon. To a casual observer, they appeared carefree. Yet underneath the surface there was a sorrow that would not leave. A need to live life quickly, a time past the giving of roses. They knew they had only that day and not the promise of another.

"So, will you accept my offer to return to Galveston and spend the night in a beach house?

Karen looked at him and smiled. A smile without a commitment.

John assumed that her smile, however faint, meant yes. "I will need to contact a realtor since my friend has let a business partner have his place for the weekend." John used his smartphone to look up realtors in Galveston County. After calling two agents, he found a rental that fronted the beach. It was located on the west end of the island and was remote from other cottages.

John put down his phone. "Karen, I have a place. It is called Sea Dreams. Will that be okay with you? It has three bedrooms and two baths with a common area between the bedrooms. There is even a screened-in porch facing the sea."

"John, are you sure that you want to do this? I know you are used to so much more in a person than I have to offer. Will you wake up the next day and regret our time together?"

John said softly, "Karen the only thing I will regret is if you do not accept my invitation. Regarding our having sex, I will go no further than what you want. The physical aspect of a relationship is not as meaningful to me as it once was. Cancer has now placed me in the realistic morning hours that you referred to earlier."

Even though John had a tendency not to speak as literally as her former husband, she understood how he felt.

"Now James," said John loudly as he smiled at him, "what would you like to do?"

"Galveston! I want to go to Galveston."

John laughed. "The Captain has spoken, and so we must do as ordered. In return, I expect plenty of sun and tons of smiles." He then turned his attention once more to Karen. "Do you want to eat out tonight at a more fashionable restaurant?"

Karen looked at him intently as though questioning the wisdom of her former reply. "John, there is too much for me to do this afternoon. Please don't be upset if I don't accept your dinner invitation. James and I need the time to get prepared for tomorrow."

"Okay, that is not a problem. Like you, I also have plenty to do."

AFTER LETTING KAREN AND JAMES OFF AT THEIR LODGING, John did not know what to do with the remains of the day. Had he acted too rashly? Was his invitation for the three of them to spend the weekend at the beach too hasty? Even though he did not love Edna, he missed her carefree attitude. He thought about Lake Travis and the moonlight on the water as the vessel sailed among the reflections of the stars.

After driving aimlessly for a short time, he decided to call his mother and father. He wondered if Edna had talked to them upon her return. As he dialed their number, he sensed that he had made a mistake.

"Hello, Mom, just wanted to check in with you and Dad. Hello? Are you there?"

A silence followed.

"Yes, John, we are here. I put the phone on speaker so your dad can hear you, too. Is that okay with you?"

"Sure, that is fine. How have you two been?"

"John, we heard from Edna. Seems like you two didn't get along as well as we had hoped."

"What do you mean by 'we had hoped'? Were you two involved in her coming to see me?"

"Yes, we were. At first she was hesitant, but we thought that if anyone could make you come to your senses, it would be Edna. You know we think the world of her and the Mancini family. They have been our best friends for at least two decades."

"Come to my senses? What are you talking about?"

"John," his mother continued, "it is obvious that you are falling for someone unacceptable. She is not a Catholic, and you refused to mention her family nor did you tell us what she did for a living. For all we know, she is married or divorced and already has a family. This is not acceptable to us."

"Dad, could you make Mother understand that I am dying? Why on earth does it matter who my friends are now? Will it take away one day, one month, or even a year of my life if I date someone below our social class?"

"John, can you hear yourself talk? Every day matters to a Johnson. We are not a family that pays homage to sickness nor do we use it as an excuse to do things that are not worthy of the family name."

"Are you kidding me? My grandfather was no more than a modern-day robber baron with a degree of sophistication. Is he the example you want me to follow?" asked John.

"You better listen carefully to what your mother is saying or she will ensure that any trust fund in your name will go to the Church," said his father almost shouting.

"Why can you not understand my medical condition? Of all people, you are a doctor. Do you think a trust fund means anything to me now?"

His mother spoke in a softer voice. "John, we love you and want the best for you. You need to come home when your treatment is over. If, and I say if, something bad does happen in the future, you will want Mass to be said by Father O'Conner. He has known you all of your life. You have always considered him as a person you can trust. Now I am even afraid to mention your affair to him. I hate to bring this up, but Edna, if you married her, would see to it that you get buried among your own people."

"Is that my goal in life – to be buried among my own people?" John could feel the anger growing within him.

"Yes, that is what is important! Don't you remember the small cemetery in Inishbofin where unbaptized infants were buried? They were not, if you recall, allowed to be buried next to the faithful, that is, their parents."

His father spoke sternly. "Your mother is more religious than I am, but I have to agree with her. Why take a chance on eternity? What if she gets pregnant? What will happen to your child? He would not be allowed to even see us."

"What on earth do you mean? Do you think that with the amount of radiation and chemotherapy I have received that I would even be capable of fathering a child?"

There was a prolonged silence over the phone. Neither John nor his family had ever considered the implications of his dying childless. Yes, there had been threats of cutting off his trust fund and leaving him penniless, but the cold, heart-breaking fact of dying without a child pierced all of their hearts.

He could hear his mother crying as she gently hung up. Despite his own desire to be free of their unending advice, he understood their feelings. In the darkness of his apartment, he lit a cigarette and stood on his balcony listening to the sounds of the city. An ambulance blared past his apartment followed by a fire truck. Soon two police cars passed with flashing lights. With the progression of the night, the city became quieter, yet in the distance he could hear ambulances racing to the hospitals that surrounded the city of cancer.

WHEN HIS ALARM SOUNDED AT FIVE O'CLOCK, John realized he had gotten far too little sleep. He sat on the edge of his bed as though waiting for someone to help him up. His illness left him with low points of energy during the day. Fortunately, the afternoons were the worst for him. He struggled to make coffee and almost fell into the recliner while waiting for the coffee to be ready.

He wondered if Karen and James were awake. He knew that she needed to feed him at night. "She too must be exhausted," he thought. "I am tired, but I am not going to let that pilot my day. I want to see them both happy. I have no other objective in life.

After leaving Karen and James at the Center, he had driven to the store to purchase as many fun things as he could comfortably load into his SUV. He did not know what the beach house had so he purchased floats, beach chairs and umbrellas. In addition, he bought some inflatable animals for James to play with in the small tidal pools that form along the edge of the surf.

He could not, however, dismiss the warnings of his parents. Deep down he felt that what they said was true. He was forsaking everything that he had known. The security of his family and his faith.

John knew that Karen had many fine attributes. She was an attractive, educated media specialist. Her attitude was very positive despite her circumstances. After his experience with Edna, he wondered about her need for him. Was it just companionship or financial support? It seemed logical to assume that she could not genuinely care for him. He was only a well-intentioned stranger to her. "But what is she to me?" he wondered as he drove to pick up Karen and James. Was she his last grasp at normalcy? Was she simply someone to talk to or someone to care for him once his conditioned worsen?

Deep down, he knew that he cared for her. He could not define what the term 'love' was. He could only feel an upwelling of emotions when he was with her. Even though they had not made love or kissed other than on the cheek, he felt that her touch would be like rain to a barren desert, a life-giving source of strength.

WHEN HE PULLED UP TO THE HOUSE, Karen and James were waiting for him. James in his stroller wearing shorts and Karen in a yellow dress that fluttered in the strong Texas wind. She wore a wide-brimmed white hat that contrasted with her tan.

"Good morning, Karen," he said as he lightly kissed her cheek. Then he turned to James. "Mate, are you ready for a sea adventure? I see that you are dressed to climb the ratlines. Yessir, ready to take the wheel of a brigantine bound for Jamaica."

James laughed at the exaggerated language. He did not understand what John was talking about, but he could sense the emotion expressed. John bent down and kissed his forehead. James looked up and smiled at him from his stroller. He then stretched out his arms for John to take him.

After securing him in the car seat, Karen sat in the front with John. He loaded the directions to the beach house in his GPS and entered the heavily trafficked lanes congested by the need of others to escape the city for the weekend.

As they drove, Karen asked if he would cut the air-conditioner off. "James likes to feel the wind and so do I. I love the breath of the approaching sea."

John looked at her. "No problem. I too like to feel the freedom that the wind conveys." He placed his hand on hers as they drove among strangers towards a dream they now shared.

"When we arrive, we should get as many hamburgers as we can eat and take them to the beach house. I am sure that it has a picnic table."

Karen looked at him smiling. "James is so happy. He will probably want two of them. Of course, he will really only play with the food."

"That is fine. There will always be seabirds willing to share his meal. I have never met a gull yet that did not love a good sandwich."

After arriving on the island and buying their lunch, they continued on towards the beach house, each one dwelling in their own dream.

CHAPTER 8

The Beach House

THE BEACH HOUSE RESTED SEVERAL HUNDRED FEET from the asphalt road. As they drove up to it, it was apparent that they had been most fortunate. It sat facing the Gulf of Mexico. The large screened-in porch also faced the sea. Perched on its pilings, it looked like a large seabird. Small ornamental palm trees flourished in the sandy yard. John picked James up from his car seat and carried him up the stairs to the paneled den where he sat down in a large leather chair still holding the toddler. James continued to grasp the small dinosaur that the old man at the Center had given him. Missing from his right hand was the wooden toy from his father.

Later, in the shade of the house, Karen and James sat together on one side of the picnic table while John sat opposite them. He was careful not to obstruct their view of the surf. The scent of the ocean was everywhere. High above the seagulls rode the strong currents of air while sandpipers ran along the shoreline marked by foam. Small shells sparkled on the beach, a reminder of the falling tide.

"This is delicious," said Karen. "I have never tasted anything better than this." She smiled, winking at James.

"Pure mate food, Lady Pirate." John laughed. He knew she wanted James to eat as much as he could, yet he only nibbled at the meat after having removed it from the sandwich. Seagulls immediately noticed their presence. Soon the birds were diving lower and lower towards the table.

James took a portion of the bun and tossed it towards the summer clouds. He could not throw very far but the strong sea breeze seemed to lift the bread higher and higher into the air. The gulls adjusted their flight path and accommodated James as he laughed with joy at their antics.

John felt that at this moment, his life was everything he had hoped it would be. He thought of a line from a movie that he had seen years before: "We have not missed it, you and I."

He wanted to hold them both tightly, protect them from harm. John was beginning to define love not through words, but through the emotions that he felt deep within himself.

"Karen, let's walk on the beach. The air is now cooler and we can talk. I would really like to get to know both of you better. To me, walking is a liberating experience."

"John, that is a great idea. Unfortunately, the stroller will not work on the sand. Are you willing to help me carry him?"

"I don't mind if Pirate James doesn't."

James looked at him and smiled, or at least John thought he did.

THE SAND FELT GOOD UNDER THEIR FEET. At first, Karen carried James who snuggled against her shoulder occasionally raising his head to look at John, not as a stranger, but as his father.

Karen glanced at John. "You may not have guessed, but James and I don't have much time left to be together. The doctor only gave him a 25% chance of living for two years. We have to make the most of it. I take more risks now with my own life – for James' sake. I have also learned to take things one day at a time and expect very little."

"Karen, I too have only a short time."

"But you look so healthy," she said, glancing at him.

"Thanks, but I am afraid that several doctors have not given me any encouragement. Let's live for today and not for tomorrow. We cannot change what is, so it is better if we accept it." He put his arm around her tiny waist.

John was still carrying the small inflatable dinosaur in his other hand. "Look, there is a small tidal pool there. Let's see if this tyrannosaurus can float." John bent down and placed it on the surface of the water. As the wind moved it, it glided over some shells and came to rest against a sand dollar.

"Karen, we have all been blessed by the sea gods. This sand dollar is whole, which means that the one who picks it up will have good fortune."

"John, what on earth are you talking about? You are simply making this up," she teased.

"Lady Pirate, it is true. I swear on Neptune's beard. A pirate who served with Blackbeard would rather have found a whole sand dollar in a tidal pool than a gold doubloon inside a sea chest."

Karen laughed. "Whatever you say, Captain."

John looked at James. "Now let's see who should pick up that treasure. I think I am too strong and might crush it. Your mother is too tall and can't bend over to see it. Why, bless me, that leaves only you James. Can you pick it up? Remember not to break it though. You need to be very gentle."

Karen lowered James to the edge of the pool. James squatted and very gently gathered the small sand dollar.

"Bless the saints and all of my Irish relatives, he just got a lifetime of good luck, so I swear by Neptune's beard!"

James carefully handed the shell to John. "Now, sir," John said, "I will put the shell in my pocket and if you ever need good luck for any reason, we will show the sand dollar as proof that your wish must be granted."

Karen took John's hand and squeezed it. He held her hand tightly and carried James in his other arm. He felt that he belonged there on the beach that stretched into the misty horizon. The sun felt warm and embracing just as her hand did in his.

James smiled at him as they strolled down the beach. John looked at him. "Skipper, let's get really wet. Karen, do you mind?"

"No, but what about you? You will definitely get sunburned without a hat and shirt on. I have already put suntan lotion on James. Besides, he has a cap on."

"Don't worry. I have been worried enough in life. I am ready for the sun to shine brightly upon me. It is time to be alive. The only regret that I have now or shall have is that I did not do this years before."

With John carrying James, they waded, into the Gulf. The sand was sucked from beneath their feet with each pounding wave. The sun sparkled on the surf and upon them. James laughed as they splashed in the warm waters of the salty sea.

John held James out so that he could pretend to swim. Perhaps he really did. More than father and son, they became one if only for a moment.

CHAPTER 9

A Simple Ending

JAMES FELL ASLEEP AS JOHN CARRIED HIM back to the beach house. Not from his illness, but from being in the sun just like any other child after a day at the beach.

"John, it is James' naptime. This has been quite a day of adventure for him. I don't think he has ever been happier in his life than he is now. I'll just put him on the daybed on the porch and be right back."

He watched her walking down the beach, the sea quickly erasing her footsteps.

John looked at the great swells now crashing on the beach as though a storm nested in the Caribbean soon to fly towards Galveston. He turned his head towards Karen when she returned. "Is there any way I can help you?"

"No, I put cushions around him so he should be safe. He will probably sleep for an hour or so."

"I love that little boy," John said. "I really do."

"I know you do," replied Karen. "I know he loves you, too. I see it in his eyes."

"Now I see why I am here. Perhaps my illness and entire life have led me to this single moment on the beach. You see, I have never known selfless love, only love wherein wealth and prestige are encapsulated in a love-of-self. So many gifts remained unseen to me. Now, because of you. I understand it was always so simple."

"John, I hope you never leave us. You have given us both such a gift. I had never hoped to know a person so unselfish in his love."

"Whatever time remains for James and me, I want it to be with you. Even if it must end so quickly, I now know that I am alive and that I have a family, a love greater than I could have ever known." At those words, Karen and James rose from the table and held each other tightly.

Two hours later, James awoke. "Daddy, Daddy!" he called from the porch.

"James, your mate will be right there," said John who skipped two steps at a time to reach the porch door. When he touched the handle, he was so short-winded that he paused for a moment to breathe deeply, but did not say anything. As he picked up James, he said, "I love you."

James replied, "I love you too, my pirate friend."

As the evening fell, they walked towards the moon that had just risen above the sand dunes. James pointed ahead and, in a barely audible voice, said, "Wait here, I must get the moon for you and Mom."

John held James in one arm while he put his other arm around Karen. Together they journeyed together towards the moon.

EPILOGUE

In the all-too-brief years that followed, the little boy painted a picture. Yes, it was only child art, rudimentary by nature and nothing special to the world, but it depicted the moon and the sea. More importantly, it featured three people: a mother, a father, and a little boy – the way life should have been, the way James wished it to be.

The Tribe of Noah

Dedicated to
James Allison King

CHAPTER 1

Nomads

ANNA, AN ATTRACTIVE MIDDLE-AGED WOMAN OF THIRTY-SEVEN, stood before the open balcony doors of her rented seventh-floor suite. Her gin and tonic sat on the table. Her aqua-green professional suit fitted tightly over her Spanx. Anna's dyed blond hair was pulled firmly into a ponytail that tended to make her facial expressions professional yet severe. She thought about the words of a friend who, having noticed that she no longer smiled, had said, "Where there is no laughter, love has fled."

Anna had traveled to Santa Monica, California to address a writer's conference. Her outward self-confidence was apparent to any audience. She was a woman who commanded attention from both men and women.

She missed her children and wished that they had traveled with her to the presentation, but the boarding school schedule in Charleston prevented them from accompanying her. Her ex-husband was a successful New York City attorney. There had been no place for Anna or the children in his life. When not at the office, he was out of town with clients, working on yet another case. His ambition and her lack of constant support for his work had led to long distance quarrels on FaceTime and Skype. In both of their opinions, a divorce could not have been prevented.

She knew how fortunate she was in life despite all the obstacles she had encountered. Still, there was something missing, something from the past that she wanted to recover.

The ocean was calm below her as the sun descended on its journey above the distant Pacific swells. It was a cloudless late afternoon, the sky changing colors quickly in the hazy twilight.

At first, Anna thought of her book that had just made *The New York Times* Best Seller list. It was a simple romance novel, the kind that always ends well. Yet she knew life was not like that, only the desire that it be so.

Below her, a bright green VW bus from the 60s pulled into the parking lot – out of place among the collection of Mercedes, Lexus and other automobiles that revealed the veneers of their owners. She remembered a summer long ago when she was young, the freedom to search for meaning in her life with little or no consequences. A time when she was lost, but had found happiness for a brief moment. Perhaps it was only a dream that she now recalled.

IT WAS RAINING HEAVILY THAT NIGHT at a truck stop just outside Charleston. It was a nondescript building with its myriad gas pumps and grease-oozing restaurant. A large sign on the roof flashed LOST HORIZON in red letters. She had walked there from the interstate after having hitched a ride with a trucker from Charleston. Dripping and cold, she entered the truck stop and found the mirror in the women's restroom. There before her reflection, she looked at herself, wet and afraid. Even though just 19, she looked much older than she was. Drugs had taken its toll on her. Once fresh, her face was now swollen and lined.

"What am I to do? I can't go back to the rehab center. My mother and stepfather have thrown me out of their house," she said to the mirror. Even though her family was prominent in Charleston society, none of their friends would have anything to do with Anna. Tears filled her eyes as she turned from the mirror and walked into the restaurant past the racks of wine and whiskey that lined the shelves of the truck stop.

Men glanced at her and quickly looked away. It was past two in the morning. Exhausted, they were there only to drink coffee and smoke – men living on nonprescription drugs to keep themselves awake. If they could just make it past dawn, they could keep driving.

"Honey, what do you want me to get for you?" said the waitress with an oversized nametag.

"Lilly, how about a new life? Isn't that why people come to a place called Lost Horizons?"

"Are you kidding?" Lilly smiled.

"You know, Shangri-La," said Anna.

"Oh, you are the first in here to make that connection. You want a new life for the price of a cup of coffee?" said Lilly, smacking her gum. "You sure know where to pick a place for advice. The people in here are too damn tired for philosophy, and I don't think there is a counselor in the lot. By the way, do you have the money to pay for a cup of coffee? The reason I ask is that you don't have a purse or wallet with you. Besides what woman doesn't have a cell phone these days?"

"Just skip the coffee. I don't have any money."

"Well, you see those three dollars that some poor truck driver just left as a tip? I will get you a cup of coffee and take it out of that."

"I can't believe you are so kind. Someday, I will repay you."

"Honey, just remember me in your prayers – that will be enough. So far I haven't had any prayers answered." Lilly looked more carefully at Anna. "You need to take better care of yourself. I swear you look a mess. I imagine you clean up really pretty-like."

NOAH AND STEVEN WERE SEATED BEHIND ANNA. They could not help listening to the conversation. Noah was a tall, broad-shouldered man with graying blond hair while Steven was shorter with thick black hair. Both men, like the other visitors in the Lost Horizon, wore the faces of exhaustion.

"Steven, it sounds like we have a compatriot sitting in front of us," said Noah with a yawn.

Noah turned around and peered at the booth behind him. "Miss, you probably haven't eaten in a while. Would you like to join us? I will split my breakfast with you. You aren't a vegetarian, are you? Because I like bacon and eggs."

At first, Anna looked away, but she could not ignore the mouth-watering odors of the Deep South breakfast that had just been served. After a moment's pause, she smiled. "Okay, I am hungry."

"Well, young lady, just come right over and join us."

Anna rose from her damp seat and sat beside Steven who reluctantly moved over.

"Rain and more rain all along the Atlantic seaboard. I think that I-95 is a boat canal. Oh, excuse me, I am Noah and the quiet reflective one is Steven. Where are you headed? Couldn't you have waited until daylight?"

Anna looked at Noah intently as though searching for the meaning of his kindness. "Believe it or not, I don't know where I am going."

"Well honey, you joined the right tribe," Noah said as he divided the eggs, bacon, and toast evenly between the two of them. "Now I will also split a cup of coffee with you. You can have my refill."

"It is nice to meet two knights in a truck stop. I assume your horses are stabled nearby."

"Oh, yep, the stallion is full of gas and ready to go. That is if he cranks." Noah laughed.

"Tell me about your horse. Is he fast and black like in books?" asked Anna whose coffee cup was now marked with her bright red lipstick.

"Nope, he is a rust-colored green, just barely travels the minimum speed on the interstate. If there is a hill, he may not even make it at a gallop."

"Well, I have a habit of picking losers for my knights," said Anna as she looked away towards the whiskey and wine bottles that waited from the nearby shelves.

"Now finish your breakfast before I take it back. You know you will have to cover the tip," Noah said smiling.

Steven looked at her. "As soon as you have finished eating his breakfast, Noah and I need to get going. I have a gig waiting for me in New York City."

"Oh, are you one of those performing types?" asked Anna.

"Yes, and before you ask, I play the sitar," Steven said, his facial expression conveying his annoyance at her condescending attitude.

"You are kidding me! You must be a major hit in the drug culture. I bet you were even in an ashram in India," said Anna with the voice of careless exhaustion.

"Yes, I was. I caught a little communicable disease and was asked to leave."

"Please tell me you are not infectious."

"Only if you are a male," Steven said avoiding any eye contact.

"Oh," replied Anna.

"Well, Anna," said Noah. "I guess I am the only one you might have to fear. I am way too old, however, to be a threat at thirty. I also have what they call a rising PSA, about the only thing that does these days." He looked into her eyes with a reassuring smile. "I tell you what, since I take in strays, do you want to ride with us to New York? I am going to drop off the serious one there and continue on to Provincetown, Massachusetts... or I think it is in Massachusetts. Hell, it might be in Rhode Island."

"Why Provincetown? I would have thought you and this sitar player would be heading for LA. You both seem the type. Oh, I forgot, they closed Route 66."

"Well, at least Provincetown, according to the map, is as far out in the ocean as I can drive. You see, I am kind of drawn to the edges of the flat earth," Noah said.

"If I wait here some more, do you think I will get a better offer?" asked Anna.

"Oh, you will get an offer all right, but it will not be for a ride," said Noah.

AS THEY LEFT THE TRUCK STOP, Anna placed Lilly's previous tip on their table. She did not know what to expect as far as the promised transportation was concerned. In her mind, she pictured a red Camaro.

The rain fell in sheets as they ran in the semi-darkness towards the stallion. Anna paused. "You are shitting me? That is what you are going to New York in?"

"Now wait a minute, just because it looks like Don Quixote's horse, Rocinante, doesn't mean it can't travel the steppes of Spain or to the ends of the earth."

"Is that the name of your VW hippie bus? Rocinante?"

"Yep, and other names when it doesn't crank."

"My god, you two are fucking hippies. Well, I guess I don't have a lot to lose," she said as rain streaked her hair and dripped onto her cheeks.

"None of us do," Noah said, shielding his eyes from a nearby flash of lightning. Thunder roared across the parking lot.

Anna opened the front passenger door and slammed it with so much force that the glass shook. Steven slid the side door open and entered more quietly as Noah closed it behind him. They sat in silence as though waiting for a church service to begin. Rain pounded on the fiberglass roof of the bus as wind shook the sides. The only illumination was the flashing LOST HORIZON neon and streaks of horizontal lightning.

Steven sat in the back of the VW in front of a caged parrot. Anna said laughingly, "What is this fucking bus, Noah's Ark?"

"Oh, you mean, Oracle. He is a conversational bird. His vocabulary exceeds that of many of my former students."

The bus entered the interstate, its wipers slowly moving. Soon Anna and Steven were asleep, too tired to worry about their destination or the stranger driving them. Noah stared at the passing lights and the few working bus gauges with the same attention as a pilot commanding a transatlantic flight.

Soon morning light broke over the small farms and suburban plaque that clogged the narrow artery of the interstate.

"Anna, tell me about yourself," said Noah.

Anna ignored his question and quickly changed the subject. "What kind of a radio do you have?" she said while changing stations. "I can't find anything on the dial except old men talking about politics and religion."

"Oh, it is an AM radio. The top rung of the antenna is missing."

"You are shitting me?" she said loudly. "I have hit bottom."

"Can you think of another expression to convey your thoughts?" said Noah as though correcting a freshman's work in one of his former English classes.

Anna fell into a resentful silence. Stretching out her body on the uncomfortable seat, she closed her eyes and mumbled, "Asshole."

Steven continued to snore loudly from the backseat while exhaust fumes penetrated the rust of the engine compartment on their flight into the interior of the vehicle.

"Say, Noah, are you sure your friend and Oracle are okay? They've been sleeping a long time."

"Anna, don't worry about them. The carbon monoxide and the roar of the engine are like a sedative mixed with Tennessee bourbon. You sleep soundly, but wake up to one god-awful headache."

HOURS PASSED SLOWLY AS THE BUS TRAVELED through North Carolina. Noah would stop occasionally on the shoulder of the road to fuel up on the cheap gasoline he had funneled into large cans and carried on top of the roof. When the need to use the restroom arose, they stopped at truck stops. These respites from the highway gave Noah the opportunity to read the graffiti above the urinals, like "Tap three times if interested."

As they traveled, Anna noticed a large billboard that read CAPE HATTERAS, THE PASSPORT TO THE REST OF YOUR LIFE. Below the large sign was a painted red arrow indicating that an exit to the beach was fast approaching.

"Noah, let's see Cape Hatteras," said Anna, staring at him with a smile.

"Cape Hatteras! That is out of our way. Besides, Steven needs to get to New York."

"If he asks, why don't you tell him that Cape Hatteras is a short cut to New York? I doubt he even knows where it is. Besides, by the time we get there, he'll just be waking up."

"Okay," replied Noah. "I have always wanted to see the cape." Noah exited I-95 near the Virginia border and headed east. The bus rode the undulating waves of asphalt towards the Atlantic Ocean.

"Hey, Noah," said Steven drowsily, "when you see a phone booth, pull over and let me make a call. I don't remember the name of the theater or where my gig is. I need to call my friend to find out."

Anna laughed. "Good luck finding a phone booth. How old are you, Steven? There are no phone booths left in the fucking world."

"Okay, Noah, pull into the next bar you see. I will make a call there. Every bar has a phone so its drunken patrons can call a cab.

Probably a federal or state law," shouted Steven above the noise of the wind and engine.

Noah soon pulled onto an access road that led to a honky-tonk surrounded by weeds and fronted by gravel.

"Stay here, I'll be right back," said Steven as he waited for Noah to open the sliding door from the outside since the inside handle was broken off.

Anna and Noah watched him walk slowly across the gravel towards the bar's entrance. Wiping the sleep from his eyes, Steven vanished into the dark interior.

"Noah, does Steven have AIDS?"

"How the hell should I know? I haven't known him more than two hours longer than you have. He does look pallid and very much underweight. I have only one mission and that is to drop his skinny ass off in New York. I owe his brother that. It is the least I can do for a buddy that kept me afloat in the Gulf of Tonkin. No one else offered to do it."

"You say that Provincetown is on the ocean. What are you going to do there except stare at the beach girls?" asked Anna.

"Well, you see, I have written a book of poetry. I want to recite my poems and hope that people will show some interest in buying one of my books or at least place a coin or two in the hat. So far I have not been able to sell a single copy of anything I have written. I think I know what the problem is. I haven't had any marketing strategy."

"Now that is a great plan – a marketing strategy for a book that hasn't even sold one copy," she said sarcastically. "Do you think anyone gives a shit about poetry? I haven't read a fucking poem since I was in school."

"Well, Anna, you do ask philosophical questions. I assume you must know a great deal about literature."

"Yes, I do. I was an English major at Sarah Lawrence until a dog sniffed my room. Apparently my roommate got jealous that I flirted with her boyfriend. She was doing drugs too, but she claimed the stash in our room was all mine. I must admit that I did fail the drug test later on that evening. That nailed a conviction, well, a misdemeanor for me. My stepfather represented me before the judge. I was, of course, asked to leave Sarah Lawrence. Their fucking loss, not mine."

Steven returned to the bus. "Shit! Man, I am fucked. The phone's been disconnected at my friend's house. How the hell am I going to get in touch with him?" Steven stared at his own reflection in the bay window of the bus as it bounced back onto the four-lane road.

SOON THE TREES BEGAN TO GET SMALLER and coastal scrub appeared. The bus crossed over the first body of water on its way to the barrier islands. Fresh sea air entered the cloistered cell in which they rode.

"Where are we going?" asked Steven.

"Does it matter?" responded Noah.

Noah found an abandoned weekend cottage road and followed it to a secluded beach. He parked the bus on a bed of seashells that crunched beneath the wheels. Before them was the end of the earth, the Atlantic Ocean.

"Noah, do you have any pot in the ark?" asked Anna.

"My poetessa, are you kidding? Do you know what is written on the side of any VW bus? It says POLICE, SEARCH HERE FOR

DRUGS. I can't tell you how many times I have been pulled over and the vehicle searched. They even had one of those damn German Shepherds sniffing through everything in the bus including me. No way am I going to have drugs in this bus or any drug paraphernalia. Nossir."

Anna sighed. "It is going to be a long evening."

They unpacked the bus near the edge of the high tide that was carefully marked by the sea's flotsam: beer cans, Styrofoam cups, and nylon line interlaced with fishhooks.

"I will pop the top to let in more air," said Noah.

"What do you mean by 'pop the top'?" asked Anna.

"Sorry, it means raise the roof to let in the sea breeze. It also allows me to stand up when using the Bunsen burner."

THE SKY WAS FILLED WITH BILLOWING SUMMER CLOUDS that wore swimsuits of orange, yellow, green and red, beautiful warm-weather clouds nurtured by the Gulf Stream. The smell of the sea filled their lungs and fueled their excitement at having arrived. It was good to finally stop vibrating against the hard vinyl seats while looking at a countryside that held no meaning to them. It was the isolation of indifference.

In the back of the bus, next to the parrot, was a crate holding some books and papers. A piece of gray metal protruded from it. "What is that?" asked Anna, pointing to the box.

Noah replied, "Just some memorabilia from my office days."

"No, I mean that metal thing jutting out from the top of the box."

"Oh, that is my dad's old Olympic typewriter. He used to be a typing teacher in the 1950s," Noah said.

"Don't you have a computer?" inquired Anna in a teasing manner.

"What on earth for? Internet costs while an old upright Olympic doesn't cost a thing except for the gas required to tote it around," responded Noah.

"Don't you keep in touch with friends and family?"

"Well, to be honest, I don't have either," replied Noah as he looked at the surf whose white crests wore the reflections of the western sun.

"I used to write when I was at Sarah Lawrence," Anna said pensively. "My English teacher even thought that some of what I wrote was good, maybe even publishable. Would you mind if I occasionally used your typewriter? It should work well on the fold-down table built into the old stallion, I mean, Rocinante."

"Sure, my dad would be happy that someone is using it again. I write my poems in a ledger using his fountain pen – you know, the kind that uses India ink and requires a blotter."

"Wow, you must really be nostalgic. Did you love your dad?"

"Of course I did. I was always a little afraid of him. Perhaps a better way to put it is that I didn't want to disappoint him. I still feel like he and Mom are alive. Watching and expecting me to finally get my shit together. What about you?"

"Oh, my mom, dad, and stepfather are all very much alive. I have one of those real extended families. Growing up, my mom was in rehab most of the time for both alcohol and drug addiction. My real dad is a doctor and a very successful lawyer in Charleston. Can you imagine a better way to make money than on medical malpractice suits? My parents are now divorced. My current stepfather owns a shipping company in Charleston. My so-called parents are real upper-crust assholes who never had time for me."

"I am sorry, Anna. My parents had no money, but at least I was loved," said Noah.

Stephen, who had been walking down the beach, returned and squatted on the sand.

"Steven, tell us about your tragic childhood," said Anna.

"What tragic childhood? I never had a childhood. I have no idea who my father was. My mother, assuming she was my mother, said he was a drunk off a freighter in Norfolk. Judging from how I turned out, he must have been a real creep. At least you know who your parents are. Can you imagine not knowing even that?" said Steven, looking at a sand dollar partially buried in the sand. He reached down to pick it up.

"Steve," said Anna, "if it is whole, you will have good luck."

Steven handed the perfect sand dollar to Anna after having brushed the sand off it. "Now I am passing my good fortune on to you."

"My friends are noble." Anna smiled as she studied his features. Steven was not handsome in a rough manly fashion, but beautiful like the cherubs on the fountains in Rome. He reminded her somewhat of the medieval paintings of Christ, men unreal in their delicacy.

"Steven, you should have given the shell to me." Noah laughed. "I am the one driving Rocinante, and I need all the good fortune from King Neptune I can get if we are going to make it to Provincetown."

"Let me see," Anna said, "I am with two hippies on a beach without any weed. And from the looks of you two, you can't afford any. I can't believe my bad luck. As my real dad would say, 'Piss-poor, Anna, piss-poor.'"

"Queen Anna, my cherub, I am sorry to disappoint you. But think how fortunate you are to see the world as it truly is once our veneers are stripped away. That is, two men who are real," responded Noah. "You may be the only woman who has ever seen two men without any pretense. Poverty unclothes us all."

"Thanks a lot, I'd rather remain delusional," said Anna. "By the way, it is getting colder by the minute. Has it occurred to either one of you to build a fire? There is plenty of driftwood. Don't tell me you two don't have any matches."

"Well, be thankful that I am always prepared since I cook my meals outdoors." Laughing, Noah produced a box of matches from his torn pants.

Soon they had a fire raging through the dry wood that they had found behind the dunes. It crackled loudly, sending sparks into the night sky where they competed with the shooting stars. Cans of soup poured into a pot were placed upon a rack that Noah had fitted above the embers.

Never in Anna's life had food tasted better to her. Warm beer was poured into lightly rinsed Styrofoam cups and then passed around. Later they lay back on the sand, each looking at the Milky Way while the moon rose above the ocean. In Diana's company were Saturn and Jupiter.

"What will happen to us now?" asked Anna. "Steven has no gig, you have no job, and I have no one but you two."

"Well, what would Don Quito say about our situation? If I may misquote him: 'Charge another windmill.' Life is full of them."

"Noah," said Steven, "Anna has a point. What will happen to us? No health insurance plan, no place of residence, no income, and no one to call for help. I would say that we are at the bottom of the cistern. Yeah, the bottom of the cistern. Right where the mud is."

"Well," replied Noah, "we have each other. That is more than I have ever had before. You know what I think? I think you two need to go to Provincetown with me. I can recite my poems, Steven can play his sitar – provided he has one – and you, Anna, can wear tight shorts and collect money from the audience."

"Are you kidding me?" said Anna, still staring at the stars above them.

"No, I am not. We will each be doing what we are most suited for."

"Now wait a minute, I don't mean to be a feminist, but I am much more than a good ass."

"Okay, we will need to figure out what you can do. In the meantime, the shorts will work best."

"Oh gifted musician, do you really have a sitar with you?" asked Noah. "I realize that I am probably joking."

"You know that trunk I asked you to put on top of the bus? It has my sitar in it."

"No kidding!" said Noah. "You mean a sitar will fit in that trunk? It must be a folding one."

"You are right again. I had it specially made for me in Calcutta. It may be the only one of its type in existence. In India, they can make steak out of an asshole. Tell you what, if Noah will help me unload her, I will play for you tonight. I don't think that either one of you has ever been serenaded by a sober sitar player on a beach. At least, I would not think so."

"Steven, that is the nicest offer I have ever received," said Anna. "I will pretend that you are my lover and that we are on a beach facing the Indian Ocean. I will wear seaweed in my hair as you play."

"Anna, you are a good audience for an old man. I would that there were flowers here for me to weave into your locks," Steven said as he assembled the instrument.

There in the glow of the campfire, the haunting music of the sitar player filled the night air. "Pancham Se Gara" mesmerized the listeners. As the fire once more became embers and the music ceased, the three of them looked at the colors of the star fields. It was like looking at a necklace worn by the sea where the stars were shades of blue, green, and red.

Constellations moved above them as the hours passed. The Seven Sisters sauntered across the summer sky as did the Hunter. Soon the full moon blotted the light from the stars and bathed the tribe of Noah in moonlight. The surf turned soft and melodic in the night. They slept as children do, safe and contented in the shelter of friends.

Noah stirred before the dawn. He looked over to where Anna had been sleeping. She was not there. Blown by the wind, her bath towel had come to rest on some sea oats. He sat up and scanned the horizon. There, down the beach, was Anna.

In the first rays of the early morning, he could see her sitting in a meditation pose, her nakedness facing the Atlantic. To him, she looked like a sea goddess worshiping the dawn. She then stretched into various yoga poses, her firm, youthful body compliant with her desires. Her naturalness was not erotic, for she appeared as a creation of the beach and the sea. For Noah to react otherwise would have broken the charm of the moment. Her modesty was protected by the spray-filled wind.

She turned and walked back to the beach unafraid, her body covered in the salty waters of the sea, sand between her toes. She shook the moisture from her hair and dressed once again in her shorts and tank top. They did not speak at that moment. It was as though she had entered his dreams, and now that he was awake, the moment was to be forgotten. And yet it could not be, for dreams nurture all realities.

The roar of the breakers broke the stillness of dawn. Light from the rising sun struck the beach and Steven who was awakened by the intensity of the newborn light.

The three continued to sit quietly knowing that never again would such a moment exist. Seagulls flew above as sandpipers rushed along the sand. Sea oats moved in the gathering wind. In the distance, surfcasters waded into the water for groupers, snappers, and sea trout; after them, the tourists would arrive from their rented beach houses. The beach that had belonged only to them in the twilight was now awake in the brilliant sun.

"I don't want to leave this beach," said Anna. "I have found a measure of peace here with you two." She patted both Noah and Steven on the back as they walked towards the bus. "Let us hope Rocinante has been rejuvenated by the beach as we have been. I think now that it is not just three of us, but four. Rocinante is one of us, shaky though she is. You know, we have all given up something to be here, and that is okay. Sometimes a lifetime is justified by a moment."

"You did not count Oracle as one of us," said Steven.

"If he ever contributes anything, I will count him in," said Anna as she looked seaward for one last glimpse of the waves and distant clouds. She did not want to let go of the peace that she now had and would, she knew, soon lose.

THEY DROVE THROUGH VIRGINIA BEACH AND INTO NORFOLK in their search for the Pennsylvania Turnpike. Without any tall buildings to guide them, they ended up passing the Little Creek Amphibious Base twice. Sailors and marines milled about the arcades or loitered around street corners.

The area was a mixture of military and tourists. The small stores filled with curiosities set among gleaming hotels promised that which could not be realized. As they drove on, there was no beauty to look upon, only the roar of the engine and an unchanging countryside.

CHAPTER 2

A Pennsylvania Farm

IT DID NOT TAKE LONG FOR HUNGER TO REAPPEAR. "Does anyone have any money?" asked Noah knowing the futility of the question. "I have just enough for gas." No one responded.

Soon they left the interstate and began traveling down a country road past horses pulling buggies. Occasionally a fast pickup would pass them defying the presence of a yellow strip. "You know, basically I am an honest person. However, Anna, you are going to have to become an actress if we are to eat."

"Not me," she said sternly. "I cannot show emotion like an actress."

"Don't worry, you just have to look pregnant. I have a sweatshirt in the rear compartment that you can put on. You just have to put some additional clothing of mine underneath it to create the desired effect."

"What on earth are you talking about? I assume that you are going to play the role of the father. No one would believe that Steven could reproduce at his age or any age for that matter."

"Well, I guess I am the father of laundry. I will double back to the large farmhouse we just past, and we will all play our roles. Just take your queues from me," said Noah nervously.

Anna laughed. "I guess it is up to me to be the leading lady. You two will definitely not be recognized by the Academy. Look at you. Noah, your beard looks like it came from a carnival makeup kit, and Steven, I don't even know how to begin to describe you."

They pulled up before the large white farmhouse with a magnificent garden facing the road. "Anna, it is necessary that you get out first. I want them to see you are not feeling well since you are pregnant. Can you act just a little sick? Don't forget how a pregnant woman walks."

Anna laughed. "Like I would know."

Noah stopped the bus next to the tomatoes. Anna got out and waddled towards the house holding her hips.

A large woman straightened up from gathering some low hanging tomatoes. "My, my, what has the road brought me today?" she said, placing her hands on her hips. Her ruddy complexion testified to long hours in the sun.

"Ma'am," said Noah. "My wife is pregnant, and I have not been able to find work. We are trying to make it back home to Rhode Island, maybe even all the way to Massachusetts where her relatives live. Can we have some vegetables from your garden and maybe one of your free-range chickens?"

"Yes, you may since you asked. Most people just steal what they want."

"Thank you, ma'am, for your kindness to strangers. The Bible says you may be entertaining angels unaware," Noah said as he and Steven began to cut okra and gather tomatoes and squash. He had never seen such tall green corn with tassels reaching for the cobalt blue sky. The sun felt warm upon their shoulders, the earth soft beneath their feet.

The farmer's wife looked at Anna. "Young lady, why don't you come and sit with me on the porch swing while your man and his friend gather what ye need? I can tell it's a boy from the position of your belly – all nice and low."

"Yes, ma'am, that is what the doctor told me. It is a boy for sure. You know, the thought of that really makes Noah happy," she said looking pensively towards him. "Me, I had rather have a girl, but the Lord knows what we need most. Noah dreams of owning a farm someday. He wants to have a son helping him. I don't mind the thought of living on a farm, especially one like this." Even though she was playing a part, she wished her words were true. To belong to someone and to have a home that was hers.

"You three are down on your luck, aren't ye? I bet you even live in that breadbox on wheels. My husband and I spent our honeymoon in a split-window bus in San Francisco. I guess that is kind of why I invited you all to stop and spend a spell with me. Kind of brings back memories – good ones. At the time you could say we were nomads. No responsibility, just living for fun. San Francisco in the '60s. Can you imagine all that? Seeing you and your husband makes me think back to those good times. What is your name?" asked the farmer's wife as she looked dreamily towards the fields of corn.

"It is Anna. My husband's name is Noah, and his friend is Steven," she replied.

"And mine is Ellen Neighbors. Since it is getting late in the day, I don't mind if you park here for the night. My husband is away on a two-week Guard duty, and it gets lonely. Just tell your men they can gather what vegetables they want along with the chicken, provided they can catch one. When done, they can bring the food up here. You and I can fix it for them."

"That is so sweet of you, but I imagine that my husband would like to get on down the road before we camp out. We are heading to Provincetown, Massachusetts, to look for work. I don't think any of our relatives will take us in. My husband keeps thinking they will. You know how relatives are. Once they get pissed, they get really pissed."

"Honey, I don't know what you are expecting in Provincetown. My husband and I rode his Harley up there several years ago. He was looking for something he could not describe. Men do that, you know. Don't go there with your dreams. That is all that I can tell you."

"I am sorry it didn't work out for you there," replied Anna.

"It doesn't for anyone. Dreams are only dreams; they are good to go to sleep with. Have you picked out a name for the boy?"

"No, I haven't. Do you have any suggestions?" asked Anna.

"Well, since your husband's name is Noah, you need to pick another Bible name. I always liked Thomas myself. One should always doubt, I say. Never take anything at face value. That is really true when choosing a man. Of course, that doesn't apply to us anymore. Right or wrong, we have already made our choice."

"I will consider that name. It is good to have a name that generates a philosophy. I would have thought that you would prefer John since his name is synonymous with love."

"My, you must still believe in love and trust. I can tell you two are in love the moment I saw you looking at each other. I don't blame you a bit, seeing what a nice smile he has. Good-looking too with his blue eyes and blond hair. Being broad and tall doesn't hurt any either."

Anna looked at Noah intently for the first time. She had never really noticed his appearance objectively. Her impressions of him had been driven by her needs to escape, sleep, and eat. It did not matter what he looked like, yet she noticed him standing there erect in the field with his hands full of vegetables. She wondered what he would look like without the reddish blond beard and long, unkempt hair.

She imagined him in a tweed coat with elbow patches lecturing an English class, the students enraptured with his discussion of Lord Byron. A campus where ivy grew freely upon the buildings and scholars gathered for conversation and tea. How far removed he was from all of that. He seemed like a defrocked priest gathering his communal food as symbolic of penitence and consequential meekness of spirit.

She then looked at Steven who was on his knees in the garden. He appeared as a weak, frail man in his early forties. While shorter than Noah, he managed to gain some height by his erect posture. His hair had been cut very close, almost as one would expect in a hospital. His color was an unusual amber and he had dark circles about his eyes. His standoffish attitude at the beginning was gone. In fact, he had become friendly with Anna, almost protective of her. She now felt that if the need ever arose, she would choose him as her confessor.

"Honey, does it bother you that Noah is a little bit older than you? I would say he is in his early thirties, and you look about twenty- three or -four. Am I right?"

For the first time, Anna realized how much older she looked than her nineteen years. Since she was no longer in treatment, she fully realized the effect that drugs had upon her health. While looking at a distant cloud whose colors reflected the late afternoon sun, she thought, "Perhaps it's time to give up what could soon be controlling me. No woman wants to look older than she really is. I can still beat the dragon. I know I can."

"Honey, come to think of it, why don't you three take the bus to the creek down in the pasture after dinner? There is clean, clear water there where all of you can bath. Nothing like cold water flowing over the body after a chicken dinner. I will lend you some kerosene lanterns for the evening," said Ellen.

"Let me ask Noah what he thinks. It certainly sounds very good to me," said Anna with a gentle smile.

CHAPTER 3

Flowing Water

NEVER HAD FOOD TASTED BETTER TO ANNA than that served by a stranger that evening on a Pennsylvania farm. After she helped with the dishes, Ellen suggested that they gather on the porch to watch the moon rise over the corn. Crickets sounded loudly while frogs sang in the nearby cattle pond. The warm smell of the fields was intoxicating. The cool evening breeze felt sensual upon her moist skin.

Anna found her body completely relaxing, a natural relaxation unknown to her. In the past, she could only calm her ever-present anxiety with drugs, alcohol, and prescription sedatives. How could the rising moon accompanied by the natural sounds of a country evening provide what she had so desperately sought?

"Ellen," said Anna, "you haven't mentioned any children. This farm seems an ideal place to raise a family."

"Anna, the Lord did not bless us in that way. I had three miscarriages. After that, the doctor said I needed a hysterectomy. It just wasn't meant to be. I do have several nieces and nephews who are like children to me. They live in nearby Phillipstown." She paused for a moment. "The Lord knows what is best for all of us. We just have to accept his will."

Anna thought that she could see a tear glistening in the moonlight. She knew Ellen would give up everything she possessed to be a mother. Anna reached over to Ellen's hand and patted it. The eyes of both women turned moist.

"I hate to interrupt our sitting on the porch," said Noah, "but we ought to get going early in the morning. We need to make some money soon or we will be in real trouble. Ellen, thank you. You could not have been kinder to us than you have been. Few people would have bothered with travelers."

"Who else will visit me if not for you? I am counting on you to stop by here if things do not work out in Provincetown. Come back anyway even if they do."

Anna looked towards her. "I will always cherish my memory of your kindness."

Noah drove Rocinante into the pasture as Anna held the gate open. As they drove further into the field, the air became sweeter as though the pasture had just been mowed – a meadow filled with wild onion and alfalfa scents. He stopped the bus just as the front tires sank into the fine sand that led to the creek. It was a flowing body of water, more like a small river than a stagnant pond. The ripples around the river stones caught the reflection of moonlight and cast it back into the eyes of the three travelers.

Noah and Steven set up the small tents while Anna straightened the foam rubber cushion in the bus. Steven then placed folding chairs around the large campfire. They were thankful that no food had to be prepared for they were very weary from having traveled so far in the bus.

Anna stood up and undressed in the light of the campfire. Steven and Noah did the same, then all three walked into the cool water of the flowing stream. There they stretched and swam.

Occasionally Anna would splash water at them in a childish game. Small lily pads grew in the still areas of the stream. Fireflies provided Lilliputian light while the honeysuckle that lined the bank cast its scent into the breeze. They breathed deeply the clean meadow air and swam gently on their backs while stars and the moon provided key and fill lights for the night stage.

Anna and Noah exchanged glances as they talked while treading water. Steven floated as an island unto himself, alone and silent.

"We three are fortunate tonight. I know this will not last. Nothing good in my life does," said Anna. "Tell me, why were you dismissed from your professorial position? Isn't that what every English teacher dreams of having?"

"I made a very foolish mistake. We all make mistakes, but few as great as mine."

"Noah, you are so serious. How does a person like you make a mistake? Everything in your life appears to be calculated, plotted, confined, and confirmed."

"Anna, I did everything right until I met the dean's wife at a party. In the south, we have lots of parties. Of course, socials are an excuse to flirt and drink. It was a hot, steamy August night. A Faulkner evening. She was standing alone when I saw her. Beautiful black hair and liquid blue eyes. I did not know who she was nor did I care when I approached her. I was single and thought nothing of flirting with any beautiful woman. It was only later that I found out she was Dean Harding's wife."

Noah continued, "I could see why she was not standing with him at the party. The Dean was a Harvard man. A brilliant, nervous type. His doctorate was in the field of Political Science. When he lectured, he always sat with his hands and legs shaking like someone on the verge of a breakdown or under tremendous stress; his face reddened as he talked."

"Knowing all of the ramifications, yet you pursued her," said Anna in the role of the prophet Nathan condemning King David.

"Are we all not foolish in our loneliness?" asked Noah. "I like to think it was only the heat of the night that drove me towards her, bewitched as I was by the dry lightning in the east."

"I guess so. You were less foolish than I. Instead of love, I sought the company of drugs. I thought that love could always be found. Of course, I did not know what I was searching for." Anna paused, then added, "We have both played the role of the fool in our lives."

Turning onto her stomach, she swam back to shore. There in the light of the dying fire and moonlight, she dressed. As Noah neared the bus, Anna went inside and lowered the mosquito netting like a door. Only the sounds of the late evening spoke.

Noah leaned back onto his bedroll and listened to the night. Deep in the woods were the voices of owls. The moon lit the stage for other night birds to call. Whip-poor-wills and northern mockingbirds sounded in the darkness while night herons stalked the shallows of the stream looking for the boisterous frogs that dwelt among the lily pads.

THE SUN AROSE EARLY AND FILLED THE SLEEPING PASTURE with light. Soon packed, the bus entered the highway with its silent, sleepy occupants. Each rider wished they could remain by the quiet meadow waters and be fed by Ellen's garden and healed by the warm sun. They too had been cast from a garden, haunted by the ever-present past.

Soon they were traveling on the turnpike past railcars, tanker trucks, and aimless highway travelers. They did not stop in New Jersey or New York except for gasoline. For lunch and dinner, they ate the homemade bread, canned peach preserves, and fresh apples that Ellen had given them. It wasn't much, but they were content. In the backseat, Steven quietly hummed a classical tune as though he were listening to an orchestra. Occasionally, he would raise his arms as though conducting his own arrangement of an unknown symphony.

In the late afternoon, they stopped just off a country road in Connecticut near one of the small streams that flowed into the tidal ponds filled with fish and wading birds. The source of fresh, clear waters that entered the bays, feeding life into the Atlantic.

When Rocinante stopped rolling and the brake was secure, they sat in silence as their bodies adjusted to the lack of sound and vibration. They unloaded the bus not far from an untraveled road that led into a hardwood forest.

"Noah, would you mind if I use your typewriter?" asked Anna.

"Not at all. Are you going to write a letter home?"

"No, just wanted to jot down some thoughts. Some notes on a book that I would like to write someday. Just trying to keep my mind active."

"The sound of clacking keys will be a new melody to the forest birds," replied Noah. "It is good to have something to occupy yourself with. I have several books I have been saving to read. I have them in my trunk on top of the bus. They are thick books that no one ever wants to read, like *The Complete Works of William Shakespeare* and Jonathan Swift's *Gulliver's Travels.* If you would like one, I will get a volume down for you."

"No, thanks. I am not that old, yet. I'd have thought that you would at least have *Lady Chatterley's Lover* and *Ulysses* up there," Anna said with a smile.

"Well, maybe I do. I am ashamed to admit that I read both of those books for the first time not that long ago. I still think that *Lady Chatterley's Lover* is not the sex novel it is portrayed to be. In fact, it is a commentary on the industrial age. The natural man versus industrialization. One time when I was first employed, I suggested that it be one of the books required for freshmen English classes."

"Are you kidding?" Anna laughed. "You sure know how to foster discontent."

"Well, you are right. The English Departmental members not only disapproved of my suggestion, but found my recommendation quite humorous."

"I can understand about *Lady Chatterley's Lover*, but did *Ulysses* make the list of required readings?"

"Seriously, no one in the department ever managed to read it. Of course, everyone knew its reputation, an unread scandalous work. No one would admit they hadn't read it. Professor Allen claimed she had. Later when I asked her if she celebrated Bloomsday on June 16. 'Of course I do,' she replied. When I asked her to explain why she celebrated the occasion, she could not tell me anything about it. Most people talk superficially about *Ulysses*, only a few know what it is truly about. Not masturbation, no! It is about life, our thoughts. We think of these things constantly, but are not condemned for them simply because they have not been written down. Anyone who has lived and been honest with himself could have written *Ulysses*," said Noah, moisture appearing on his forehead from the still heat of the day and from the emotions of his thoughts.

"I don't agree with you," said Anna. "When I read it, I imagined that each sentence was a book unto itself. I had to read it as carefully as one does the Bible. No masterpiece should be so carelessly glanced upon or summed up in two sentences."

"We all see through a glass darkly," said Noah in a dismissive tone. He did not wish to argue with someone he did not consider as his equal in literature. After wiping his brow, he continued, "I have written many professional articles. What you publish in a scholarly journal ensures your anonymity. Your thoughts will be as unread as that of poetry. Finding a reader is not the easiest of tasks. I will tell you what – I will read what you write. I will be both your friend and darkest critic."

"Impossible," said Anna as she set the typewriter on a stump and began to type, her legs firmly grasping the remains of the tree. "How can I have faith in your criticism if it is accompanied by friendship?"

Ignoring her comment, Noah said, "You are a lucky woman. That stump is level and the right height. Your thoughts must be ethereal since you do not require an oaken desk, air-conditioning, or a computer. You remind me of an impressionist painter of words."

Anna smiled. "Noah, what are you talking about?"

"You type and then you look up as though drawing inspiration from the forest. The changing light, the shadow of leaves must alter your thoughts. You are the woodland James Joyce. Bravo, well done to those that are original or pretend to be!"

Anna smiled at him as she placed another sheet of his paper into the typewriter and returned the carriage to begin typing her second page of notes. The typed words appeared very dim in the early twilight. "Noah, how old is this ribbon?"

"I don't know. Probably several years old. I will buy you a new ribbon if you write something that pleases me. Since there is not much light left, why don't you write a brief poem? You can even compose it in the moonlight if you like. If I remember correctly, Vincent van Gogh painted 'Starry Night Over the Rhone' in the darkness of night."

"Incurable romantic. It is difficult enough to write on a full stomach in an air-conditioned media center. How can I think while mosquitoes, ticks, and fleas dine impatiently on my legs? Have you ever straddled a pine tree while trying to be creative?" Anna said with a slight sigh.

"Each bite will remind you of your mortality. A writer should think only of the words that are being written. Nothing else matters. Remember that you are not here; you are with your protagonist. His thoughts are your thoughts. His pain is your pain."

"Yeah right, you are so successful at writing," Anna said sarcastically. "One half-ass book of lousy unread poetry. It seems like the insects did not improve your talent. Oh, I forgot, you had an air-conditioned office at the university. A few more nights on the road and I will be classed among the romantic poets – that is, if I can stop itching enough to write."

"Okay, okay. So I am a failure at just about everything. I too doubt if hunger will increase anyone's ability. I think that Steven gathered some cabbages from the garden. I will use the melted ice water in the freezer to boil the cabbage."

Anna laughed. "What a Polish idea. Don't they love cabbage, too?"

"If you are hungry enough, a cabbage will taste like steak or even swordfish. In the South, a crawfish tastes like a lobster when you are poor. Yes, the appetite determines the taste and pleasure of food."

"Well," replied Anna, "you need to start fattening up your friend. He is too thin."

"Anna, I see you were able to find a skirt. How in the world did you manage that?"

"Oh well, we did promise to be honest with each other. I took it from Ellen's clothesline. I have to pin it up since it's too big for me. I could have taken more clothes, but I didn't. Do you think she will ever forgive me?"

"Probably not." Noah laughed. "I will defend you. Your ox is certainly in a ditch."

"I knew you were a prophet. How else could I justify your arriving at my hour of greatest need?" Anna smiled.

"Luckily, I had the requisite ark just in time for the flood. I will busy myself looking for a stream where we can all bathe," replied Noah. He walked down the deserted road towards some very large oaks.

Steven approached her. "Anna, from the way Noah looks at you – you know, that sideway glance he gives you – I think he is falling for you. Please be careful. He has no future and is too old for you."

"Steven, are you kidding? What future do any of us have? He is still young, educated, and very good-looking," Anna answered.

"Yeah right, but what is he doing with us? You can always judge a man by his company. If I had been successful, I sure would not be here wondering what boiled cabbage cooked in melted ice water tastes like. Nossir, I would be drinking the finest Chianti and sitting at a sidewalk table near the Trevi Fountain in Rome. Instead,

I will soon be dining on a stump hoping that the water I drink will not give me typhoid or diarrhea."

"I have been to the Trevi Fountain with Mom and my real dad," said Anna, looking towards a lark whose song sounded throughout the nearby meadow. "It wasn't so long ago that I went to Europe. It was my high school graduation gift. My parents accompanied me and a girlfriend of mine. Of course, they just fussed the entire trip. Seems like my dad found Italian women attractive while my mom sampled the wines of Italy. Some trip! Damn them for being my parents! Waste, waste, fucking waste!"

"Anna, don't forget that Oracle can hear you. Noah has removed the cover from his cage, and he is now wide awake. All we need is for him to repeat, 'Waste, waste, fucking waste!' to a crowd of buyers and givers. You know, if I get any more hungry, I am going to eat that damn bird."

Anna could not believe herself, but she too looked at Oracle as a forest animal would, weighing benefit of attack against risk incurred.

"So, you think Noah is attracted to me? Well, I don't object to being flattered if it goes no further than that. The last thing I need is another failure looking sideways at me."

"You are safe," said Steven. "He is passionate from the neck up. Anything more is like expecting Rocinante to go seventy-five on the turnpike. It just ain't going to happen."

Anna could not help but laugh at his honest appraisal. Sitting herself once more at her typing stump, she stared at the off-white sheet of typing paper as if expecting an icon of the church to miraculously appear upon its yellowing surface. "Let's see, what is there to write about at this moment? Nothing, nothing, nothing!" She closed her eyes, opened them once more, and began to type.

The Faithful

A quiet stream that traces the woodlands of the field.
Flowers that present their incense to gods not seen.
Wild birds the voice of nature's faith.

The search for love's most gentle touch
Will time yield that which I seek?
Not friend, but lover found among wild things.

When Anna stopped typing, Steven approached her. "Do you mind if I read what you have written? I assume that your words are filled with thoughts of abandonment and defeat." He was silent as he read the few words that composed her poem. "Is that what you are seeking and have not found – a lover? I thought you were fleeing from a failed relationship. If so, why on earth would you seek another knowing it too will, in all probability, fail?"

Noah dropped some firewood near her and asked if he too might read her first composition on the typewriter. "Anna, my typewriter is privileged to have you use it. You are now our distinguished poet of the fields. The voice of us all among the flowers and yes, I must admit, newly discovered cow patties." Noah then commenced to eat his food while seated on the serrated edge of a recently fallen pine stump.

After Steven had tasted the boiled cabbage, he said without any intention of humor, "Now I know why the Polish flee to Ireland."

CHAPTER 4

The Carnival

"WHILE YOU TWO WERE ENJOYING A MIDSUMMER'S NAP," said Noah, "and I was trying not to fall asleep at the wheel, I noticed a sign just before exiting off the interstate. It read CARNIVAL TONIGHT IN MERRIMACK. If I read the filling station map correctly, we are only about six or seven miles from there. I have a few dollars saved back for pleasure only. Well, really for emergencies. Not much but maybe a hotdog apiece and one ride for the three of us. We haven't had any entertainment or fun for several days. What do you say about being hedonistic tonight?"

Anna could not contain her enthusiasm. "Great hallelujah, all that jazz, and whatever else is up there in the sky! I am more than ready."

Steven was less than enthusiastic. "You two go ahead. I will stay at the campsite. Someone has to remain rational and guard everything. If you don't mind, however, bring me back a hotdog and a bottle of water."

"Sure," said Noah. "Anna, let's call this our first date."

"Hey, wait a minute," Anna said with a mischievous smile. "I agreed to eat your hotdog but not to be your date. You need to be rational in your expectations. You have violated the first rule of expectation: don't expect anything."

"Oh well, I agree, one should not expect so much from life," said Noah. "I should never have hoped for a date and a hotdog in the same evening. What on earth was I thinking?"

They laughed together at the thought of simple expectations, those shared when love is new and innocence abounds in a thought.

Leaving Steven seated on a stump assembling his sitar, they climbed back into the bus and followed a tree-lined two-lane road to Merrimack.

"Well the frogs and owls are in for one fine concert tonight," said Noah, firmly gripping the oversized wheel of the bus, his ears attuned to every sound that the simple engine made. He knew they could not afford any major repairs. He had no backup plan, no one to call, or even anyone to care. But he knew all would be well for they had the greatest gift of all: each another.

As they approached Merrimack, Noah noticed how deserted the streets were that evening. Everyone, he thought, must be at the carnival. The only sound in the streets came from the rusted bus muffler that echoed off the rows of two-story brick buildings. Soon Noah saw a parking lot filled with cars. On a large piece of cardboard read the hand-printed words: PARKING $5.00. "Well, almost-date, it looks like we are going to have to park down the road and walk back. Your prophet cannot afford the fee."

Anna did not say anything about the long walk from where they had to leave the ark. Their steps took them past darkened shops and alleyways. Even the City Cafe was closed, yet the smells of French fries and hamburgers persisted in the evening air. The town reminded Noah of a deserted movie set that he had seen when his parents took him to Hollywood. It was a town of conformity, New England work ethic, and rehearsed faith.

Anna walked slightly ahead of him, avoiding any attempt to hold hands, the rules firmly established by her. As they strolled, mechanical music filled the humid air with its staccato beat. The lights of the Ferris wheel shone above the carnival while a merry-go-round occupied the heart of the former Methodist campground. The whole populace of Merrimack seemed to have been herded into the carnival by their desire for fun.

"Noah, I haven't been to a carnival since I was a little girl in Charleston. I still remember how happy I was, how I tugged on my mother's hand. I even won a doll."

"Well, I tell you what," said Noah filled with the intoxication of the moment, "I too am going to win you a doll." He knew how futile his noble words were since he had never thrown a baseball at pins carefully stacked on inverted baskets. "Anna, I am really happy tonight. I have forgotten what it was like to feel this way. *A jug of wine, a loaf of bread and thou beside me...* at a carnival."

"Noah, you continue to surprise me. I have never dated any man who can cite from *The Rubaiyat of Omar Khayyam.* It is one of my favorites."

"Does a misquoted line count?" Noah laughed.

The bridge between caution and longing was crossed thanks to a single line of poetry. The carnival night ended all formality as Anna and Noah became friends, no longer content to be indifferent strangers in a symbiotic relationship.

Noah took Anna's hand in the dim light of the street, and she allowed it. They did not release that outward sign of an inner bond until the lights of the carnival defined them in light.

An obese barker shouted, "My good man and young lady, I'll guess your weight for a dollar! Just look at the prizes you can choose from if I am off more than three pounds. Let me guess the little lady's weight."

Noah noticed how the barker scanned Anna with more than metric interest.

Noah looked at the prizes: piggy banks, monogrammed ashtrays, and ceramic ladies that functioned as pencil sharpeners.

"No, sir, not tonight. Maybe tomorrow," said Noah. He could never force himself to disappoint anyone directly or totally. There always needed to be another chance to be taken. Perhaps that explained why students always fought to be in his English class. Coeds knew that if they flirted with him, they stood a good chance of being able to repeat an exam. Not that he would give them a grade they did not earn, but that they would be allowed to try again.

As Noah looked at the crowd and circus attendants, he felt anxious for them. It was a mixture of feeling very sorry for the misfortunes of those around him and at the same time joyous exhilaration that so many events in other people's lives had not happened to him.

"Now I must win you a doll with the accuracy of my pitch," said Noah. There before them was a tall thin man seated behind a counter top. Dolls were carefully arranged on shelves behind him.

"My good sir," said the barker as he looked at Anna. "Do you have the talent to win the young lady a doll?"

"Indeed I do," responded Noah, producing the required two dollars.

"Three tries to land a ball in the basket," the barker said loudly.

Noah took careful aim and threw the ball. It landed exactly in the basket only to have it bounce back free.

"Anna, I will adjust the strength of my throw," Noah said as he studied the position of the basket. He threw the ball more lightly than he had previously done. This time he missed the basket entirely, the ball falling short. "It's just like Vietnam, you fire once over and then short. This time it will be exactly on target." He mimicked a professional baseball player with his exaggerated throw. It landed perfectly in the basket and remained there. Even the barker looked amazed.

"Sir, you are a talent indeed. Now you must pick the doll."

"Anna, which one would you like?"

"Noah, I would like the smaller one in the ball gown. Her hair looks just like Ginger Rogers'." When the barker handed it to her, Anna smiled. "Noah, you are a weaver of dreams. I ask and you provide. Perhaps you are a magical figment of my imagination."

At that moment, Anna turned towards the rows of lights being lifted above the carnival. "Look at the Ferris wheel! Noah, I love Ferris wheels. I remember the big one at the South Carolina State Fair. It seemed to go clear through the sky. Please, let us ride," she coquettishly pleaded.

Noah looked into Anna's eyes. "Sure." He found the money deep in his pocket and paid the attendant. He helped Anna into the wicker basket that rocked freely. The chair, being very small, pressed them against each other. Anna felt so warm that he imagined a force radiating from her body into his own.

He held his leg rigid to avoid pressing against her, but with the first jerk of the Ferris wheel, his leg no longer followed his rational command. Higher and higher from the ground they rose as though reaching for the night clouds that sped past the early summer moon. The sound of the carnival grew softer as the car rose. The stirring breeze, filled with the scents of mowed alfalfa hay and wild onions, gently bathed their warm summer-moistened bodies.

The lights of the small town vibrated below them in the distance. "Anna, now I know why you love Ferris wheels. They must be the coolest places in the summer. This hot humid weather is bound to brew some thunderheads," said Noah, watching the lightning in the east.

"Noah, I feel wet all over. The humidity is awful. Yet the breeze here, as you just said, makes me feel almost comfortable."

Noah gazed intently at Anna for a moment. Her eyes reflected a myriad of lights. Noah's eyes then moved to her lips. His face felt flushed for it dawned on him that he was staring at her and she was not speaking. That she too was gazing intently into his eyes stirred new emotions in him.

"I see the carnival in your eyes," Anna said as she leaned closer to alter the perspective of her vision, their glances having once more met. Involuntarily, as though by instinct rather than by reason, Noah gently kissed her lips.

Anna pulled back. "Noah, what are you doing? I can't believe you did that after I stated the rules of our relationship. Even you concurred." The tone of her voice indicated that her reproach was indeed very mild and that the evening would not be altered through the role-playing of her having been offended.

Anna leaned back and looked towards the Milky Way. "Look how gorgeous it is. Every time we go up, it looks like we are about to follow a path to the stars. Look, Noah! A shooting star."

"I saw it too. They say that if you wish upon a shooting star, it will come true. Did you make a wish?"

Anna did not respond immediately. After a brief pause, she said, "Yes, I did."

"Did it concern me?" asked Noah.

"Yes," she said quietly.

Noah did not know what to say. He felt afraid to speak as though a spell had been cast that he did not wish to end.

The Ferris wheel soon stopped. Noah and Anna were the first to get off. They began to walk toward the van and away from the sounds and reflections of the carnival. Anna touched his hand and placed it in hers. "My wish very much concerned you." Turning towards him, she said, "Isolation is my only strength. We both know this can never work. We will only hurt each another."

"Then why did you take my hand?" asked Noah.

"I needed to feel that I was not alone," responded Anna. Noah looked at her and did not reply.

CHAPTER 5

Passageway

IN HIS SLEEP, NOAH HEARD STEVEN'S VOICE: "Wake up. Man, you have slept most of the morning away. What time did you and Anna get back from the carnival?"

Noah answered in the half-light of a dream, "Steven, I have no idea, but it was not too late. I think that the carnival closed just a little after midnight. Anna and I then had a cup of coffee and came back here after that. Nothing more, I can assure you. By the way, your hotdog and water are in the icebox."

"Thanks. Are you starting to fall for her?" asked Steven.

"No, not really. My existence is too chaotic right now to take on another person's life," answered Noah.

"Isn't that what you did when you asked both of us to join you?"

Noah yawned before replying, "Yes, I suppose so. When I asked you two to join me, we all had nothing left to lose. None of us had any destination or dreams left. If you fall in love, you need to be committed. How can I commit to anything beyond this trip?"

"Hell, man. You can always teach. Sitting on your ass is always easiest when you can rationalize your position. So what if your dean won't give you a recommendation? Just don't include your last gig in your vita. If I listed everything that I did in my resumé, I would be sitting in a cell somewhere in India. I always practice safe selection when it comes to resumés. Shit, I wish I could say the same about the rest of my life. Just tell 'em what they need to know and nothing else. Leave out the juicy part that they would really like to hear, but are forbidden by law to ask."

"Steven, you do offer good advice, but you have failed to grasp the meaning of this trip. I am trying to find out what is important to me. What life is really about. Okay, that sounds like a rewrite of *Walden.* I have to admit that Thoreau is still a hero of mine. Somewhat like the father of my imagination. Do you think I would be happier in a large house than I am right now? Could I write better poems if my desk was rosewood? Nossir, I have to know what is important. All the shit around us means nothing. You and Anna do mean something however."

"Fucking Thoreau. That is what you are. Don't you get it? That is why the man left Walden Pond. He finally figured it out. There was nothing there."

"Don't talk so loud. Anna is probably still sleeping."

"Like shit she is," said Steven. "She went swimming at dawn. At times I think she is far from normal, all fucked up. What kind of a woman gets up before the sun and prays to cold water?"

"Perhaps there is something in the dawn that she is looking for."

"If there is, I sure to hell hope that she finds it."

"Steven, when she returns, let's ask her," suggested Noah.

Both men continued to lie on their bedrolls listening to the morning doves that had gathered in a nearby wheat field. Their song reassured them that life had begun again.

NOAH STARTED THE CAMPFIRE. Then he placed two large slices of Spam on the hot skillet resting on the burning wood. After putting them on a plate, he placed two pieces of bread in the grease to warm the slices. The strong smell of campfire coffee soon joined the odors that welcomed Anna back to the campsite. Dressed in her denim skirt and blue tank top, she knelt by the fire.

"Anna, did you enjoy the carnival last night?" asked Steven.

"What? Oh yes, I sure did."

"Well, what did you enjoy?" questioned Steven.

"The moon and stars were very bright above the Ferris wheel. It seemed as if I could touch them."

"Hey, did you and the captain have some pot and did not invite me to join in?" Steven laughed.

"No, we only had each other," she said, looking at Noah with a smile.

"Now let me see, what am I supposed to make of that?" Steven smiled as he winked at Noah.

Noah said, "Well, my friend Steven, I hate to disappoint you, but Anna firmly established that we are not nor are we ever going to have a sexual relationship. I do admit, however, that I did merit one innocuous kiss, no more than what you would give your brother or a friend. I can sum up my life with only one word: possibilities. Yes, that sums up it. Possibilities without accomplishments."

Anna smiled. "Expectation? It is more than what I should have given you. There are clear rules in life. When you work together, you do not screw together," she said, laughing.

"What on earth are you talking about?" asked Noah.

"Well, you did offer to have me collect money from the audience while you recite your poems and Steven plays his sitar. I consider that business and as such the rules must be respected. Absolutely no dating allowed."

"Anna, you don't have to worry about me," volunteered Steven. "Nature left me out of the running."

"Well, whatever," responded Anna.

"I noticed that you got up before dawn and bathed in the stream. Were you praying? Weren't you in one of those salutation poses when I first saw you?" questioned Steven who had suddenly become more vocal.

"You mean the lotus position. Yes, I was thanking the woods, the fields, and the water of the stream for the life that they have given unto each of us. They are the only forces I recognize."

"What about the love between a man and a woman?" questioned Noah. "Is that not a natural force?"

"Noah, first you have to believe in love. I have never known it. I pray to what I can see or have felt through my own experience. All else is an illusion to me."

"Anna, you must have really been hurt," said Steven.

"Yes, by everyone that I have ever depended upon," replied Anna.

"What about Noah and me? In some ways, you depend upon us."

"Steven, even though I care for both of you, we will eventually hurt each another. My goddesses are much more kind. They give me the scents of the meadows, the sounds of forest birds, and water to drink. Why should I not worship them?"

"I can't believe it," said Noah, laughing. "We have a druid among us. A true pagan indeed. No wonder she prays naked to water and rocks."

"Call me what you will. I am my own identity. I will not share myself with others," replied Anna.

"Even with friends?" asked Noah in a serious tone.

"Even with friends."

After Steven had once more fallen asleep, Anna turned towards Noah.

"When we were returning from the carnival, you changed."

"What do you mean?" asked Noah quietly.

"You kissed me on the Ferris wheel and, walking back to the bus, I placed my hand in yours. After that it was as though we were strangers. I think that we both felt the separation between us."

"I am sorry. I don't want to feel passionately about a person any more than you want me to. I think that we have both summed up our positions very clearly. Above the carnival last night, I simply forgot the rules. As I told you much earlier, I am to be the father of an illegitimate child I will never see. The dean's wife outwardly claims that the baby is her husband's. However, she was very honest with me. It is definitely my own. Unfortunately, the dean knew about the two of us. She had kept a note I sent her in her wallet as well as my photograph. When confronted by her husband, she claimed that some other jerk had written the note, but the dean checked the handwriting against my own. Can you believe that shit? It also turns out that he is impotent."

"But you can run a DNA test and prove that the baby is yours. That way you can have visitation rights when the baby is born," said Anna.

"What do I have to offer a child? The dean is a well-respected full professor with tenure. In addition, he is independently wealthy. He comes from a prominent New England family with a signer of the Declaration of Independence in his family tree. There can be no scandal. My child will be raised in a privileged home with a good name. I think the Irish call it being 'born into the ascendancy.'"

"Noah, you are a fool. Look at me – I too had a privileged life. Now I am with two has-beens in a fucking bus. Be honest with yourself. Someday, your baby will need you and like the selfish bastard that you are, you will not be there. I have to ask one more question: Have you given up sex out of fear or as a form of repentance?"

"Probably as a form of repentance. How else can I atone for such a great sin?

"Come now, Noah, don't tell me you have suddenly found religion. You are a man of many mysteries, but religion?"

"Are you stripping me of any sense of moral code?" asked Noah, looking into her eyes.

"Then I am to be the forbidden fruit. You see how long Adam lasted. You know I could have had you just for the asking last night. Just a touch and I would have consumed you with a passion you have never known before. You now know how I would have reacted had you touched me in that special way. All men are gullible. It just depends on opportunity."

"Your tone is like that of a black widow spider that lies in wait to consume its mate. Anna, I have to be sure this time. To make love, I must love, and that is not as easy as touching a person even if she desires it. As you will remember from your youth, Adam needed Eve, but love was not mentioned in the garden."

CHAPTER 6

Mystic Seaport

"**W**ELL, CREW MEMBERS, WE NEED TO HAVE a strict accountability of tasks. I drive and worry about the overall vision. Steven, you cook and Anna, you wash and clean," said Noah in the authoritative manner of a whaler's captain.

"Shit, Noah, don't play your role too seriously," said Anna.

After the final preparation for getting the bus underway, Noah turned the ignition switch on. Slowly the four-cylinder engine turned over, finally catching as the battery became weaker. Noah continued to pump the gas pedal hoping to keep the small engine alive as they entered the highway. Cars sped past them after honking or giving him gestures of impatience.

Suddenly the gas pedal broke. It lay limp on the floor of the bus. Immediately Noah gave a hand signal to passing cars and pulled onto the shoulder of the road. "Shit! Shit!" shouted Noah as the bus bounced on the uneven ground. He brought his head onto the wheel in a symbol of defeat. "Now just be calm, Noah, and think," he said out loud to himself. After examining the pedal, he realized that all he needed was an object to serve as the connection between the accelerator and the foot pedal. "Hey, Steven, you know that plastic Pepsi bottle you were nursing on yesterday? Throw it to me."

"Yap, Captain," replied Steven. After a quick search, he found it on the floorboard, rather flattened from his feet having rested upon it.

Noah slipped the Pepsi bottle under the foot pedal and ran several preliminary tests. "Can you believe it, crew? We've been saved by a discarded Pepsi. Not exactly the kind of repair you'd see on *Star Trek*, but it works." The bus reentered the interstate with Noah attending not only to the traffic but also the precarious position of the Pepsi.

"Noah, I have always wanted to see Mystic. Would it be possible for us to take a side trip there?" asked Anna.

Noah pretended to look at an itinerary. "Let's see if I can fit it into the schedule. After all, I have already detoured once for you. Why do you want to go there?" he asked, glancing in her direction.

"I don't know. I guess that I just love the name. It makes me imagine a port with fog and coastal sounds, the stretching of mooring lines, the utterance of ship horns, and the clang of channel markers."

"I too would like to see it. While in the Navy, I was sent to school not too far from Mystic. I never did get down there to see the port. The last thing I wanted to see was more vessels afloat. As the old timers would say, 'Put an oar on your shoulder and walk inland. Only when someone finally asks you what's that you're carrying is it safe to build a home and a life for yourself.'"

Soon Rocinante entered the narrow streets of Mystic. "Let's see if I can find some free parking. Of course, I doubt that it exists in a tourist town like this." The bus continued to pass rows of parked vehicles and car lots that charged an exorbitant sum.

"Wait, I see a spot. Oh man, shit, there is a motorcycle parked on it." Noah's voice strongly conveyed his agitation.

"Why don't we move the motorcycle so we can park there, too?" asked Steven.

"Okay. Those things weigh a ton, but it is an older bike. We may be able to put it in neutral and push it to the side."

Anna looked at them with amazement, seeing trouble ahead.

"Hey, I have an idea. Why don't we set up shop right here on the sidewalk? That way, we can watch the bus and still hone our skills. Anna, it is time to put on the short shorts," Noah said seriously.

"Are you kidding? You might as well ask me to solicit on the sidewalk," Anna replied sternly.

"Okay, okay, just stay dressed as you are. You never know, we might have to leave quickly."

"'Quickly' is not a word that applies to Rocinante, but I admire you for coming up with an escape plan," replied Anna.

They hurriedly unpacked the VW, placing the poetry books on a portable metal stand as Anna attached a wireless microphone to Noah's shirt. Steven managed, after some difficulty, to unload the sitar case with its folded stringed instrument off the roof.

Soon Steven was seated on a small stool tuning the sitar. They felt that they had picked a good location. People who had parked in the lot must pass alongside the narrow street as they returned to their cars.

Seeing a crowd of pedestrians walking his way, Noah began reciting a poem with the flare of a dramatic presentation.

Screens

Barriers to all except the common fly.
Persistent insect that flies unimpeded to the apple pie.

Screens, a symbol of the forest den.
Sunlight without and darkness within.

As a child, I entered my clapboard home.
Now others latch the screen as I depart alone.

Failed marriage and dependent son.
Maybe screens should be left alone.

As he recited the words, Steven played a short tune that he had learned while stoned in Calcutta. Music that stirred emotions, not thoughts. As the event transpired, Anna stood laughing, pressing her bucket to her side. Suddenly, an elderly man placed a ten-dollar bill into the bucket. Then three other pedestrians followed suit. All told, one brief poem with musical accompaniment had netted then fifteen tax-free dollars. Enough for a hamburger split three ways and a large Coke they could share.

Even Noah was surprised when a woman looked at one of his books of poetry and handed him a twenty-dollar bill. "Never mind the change," she said with a smile. "Would you mind signing this?"

Noah could not speak; his voice was lost in his throat. He acknowledged her request with an exaggerated affirmative shaking of his head as she produced a pen for him to write on the front page of the book entitled *Failed Marriages and Other Gifts*.

Out of the crowd appeared two Mystic policemen.

"Officers, what might I do for you?" asked Noah somewhat sheepishly.

"First of all, I want to see your permit for a street performance. I know you don't have one so don't pretend to look. Second, I wanted to save your ass by mentioning the fact that you have moved the Black Duke's bike. When he comes out of the Pirate's Den bar down the street, he will take that sitar and insert it as an enema up your ass."

"Thank you, sir. I really appreciate your thoughtfulness. I will relocate my traveling minstrels immediately." Noah managed a smile while thanking the officers who stood waiting for Rocinante to leave. Noah attempted to start the bus, but it only growled as he cranked the engine.

Suddenly, Black Duke appeared before the bay window of the bus. A tall, gray-haired, muscular man who had obviously developed his physique in prison. His face wore a handlebar mustache. Both arms and neck were covered in a variety of floral tattoos. He banged his fist on Rocinante's VW front emblem. The metal dented on impact. "Who the hell moved my bike?" he thundered.

Sweat beading on his forehead, Noah replied, "Sir, those two policemen there pulled me over for a drug check. You know how that goes." He looked the biker in the eyes.

"How did my bike get moved?" shouted Black Duke, spraying Noah's cheeks with spit.

"Well, those two policeman moved it over so that they could take their time inspecting the bus. They went through everything looking for drugs, paraphernalia, the whole damn works. When you drive a 60s bus, they assume you are guilty until proven innocent. They also thought that we were pimping Anna, can you imagine that shit? I bet they will be checking your saddlebags next."

"Those sons of bitches! When I find out where they've parked to get coffee, they are going to wish they had someone nearby to replace their tires and side paneling. Fuckers!"

After backing into the traffic, Noah paused to thank Black Duke through his open window for having offered his parting sympathy to them.

"Shit, that was close!" said Noah.

Anna reprimanded him, "Those two cops were nice, and now you have sicked the Duke on them."

"What else was I to do? Anyway, they have guns. We have only a sitar to hit him with. Besides we are off to Provincetown."

CHAPTER 7

The Business Model

"**W**HAT WE MUST DO IS PROFIT FROM OUR EXPERIENCE. What have you learned, Anna?" asked Noah.

"First, asshole, that you want to turn our adventure into a fucking classroom lecture. You're playing the professor who assigns oral reports so he does not have to think."

Noah responded, "No, Anna, if we can learn something from our first experience as a team, then we can apply it later. I cleared seven dollars on the book and you got fifteen in your bucket."

"You know what that tells me? A good ass is worth more than poetry." She smiled.

"Since you are not mature enough to respond to my academic question, I will ask Steven. Have you learned anything from our experience that you care to share with the group?"

"I've learned that Anna is the smartest member of the crew. She cuts to the chase and sees life as it really is. You and I are just the barkers; there is no talent between us. As for that poem about a screen door – are you kidding me? Try playing music to accompany that!"

"Hey, now come on, Steven. Screen doors do play a role in our lives. I just made it up as we were standing there. I couldn't find my glasses, so I was unable to read from my book of poetry. I just couldn't let such a great opportunity pass me by." Noah continued, "You know what I learned? We should setup on a street that has parking lots. Forget downtown. That way we get them coming and going with or without their spending money. People always hold back a five or so even when they are broke. Some people just want to buy anything at the end of a short trip, preferably the memento of an experience that they can talk about later. That is why my sign offers free author autograph, date, and location of purchase.

"Then there are other people who just can't stand having money in their pocket. When you have a choke point in a road, you know, parked cars on both sides of the street with lots of traffic in between, they can't cross over to avoid you. You often have the meek and timid wanting to give you money in order to avoid embarrassment. I can go on and on, but I have kind of figured out our business model."

Anna looked at Noah. "A business model of what? What on earth are you talking about? Three adults made twenty-two dollars in one day."

"Well, you can laugh if you want," said Noah. "Some rich men don't even clear twenty-two dollars in a day when you look at their debits. We have twenty-two dollars tax-free. What did the bus cost besides some gas money, and I – if I have to, but of course I won't can siphon that off from other nearby vehicles. Man, we are living for free, sort of like going west in the 1800s, only we are going east. Makes sense to me."

"Stop being so practical, Anna," Steven said looking at her ponytail blowing in the wind from the backseat window vent. "We are not in this for the money. Why do you think I spent a year in an ashram? It sure wasn't to make money. If you really came from Charleston society, I bet you have not worked a day in your life."

"Well," replied Anna, "I worked at a summer camp for children with special needs. I know what work is about."

Noah laughed. "Alrighty then, we have settled that."

Suddenly the silent parrot Oracle spoke from behind Steven. "What the fuck? What the fuck? Feed the bird."

Noah shouted over the roar of the engine, "Who has been saying that? I told both of you not to use profanity in front of Oracle. He is part of our act to attract children and as a prop for Steven so he will look even stranger. We can't have a cursing bird on the street!"

For the next twenty-five miles, Oracle continually repeated, "What the fuck? What the fuck? Feed the bird."

Noah shouted to Steven, "Put the lampshade over that fucking bird. He doesn't know how hungry I get at night thinking about him. I don't dream of girls; I dream of parrot fillets."

As they drove, the trees became smaller and they caught glimpses of the open ocean reaching into the land like fingers. Pools of stagnant, brackish water filled with shallow aquatic growth appeared. Anna slept in the cool breeze of the open window while Steven slept, contented by the roar of the engine and the inhalation of diluted carbon monoxide generated by the churning engine.

Noah thought with pride about making money doing what he enjoyed the most, reciting poetry and performing. The world belonged to him that day and no one else.

Noah adjusted the vent window to allow more fresh air to strike his face. "Anna, have you ever been to Paris?"

She yawned at having been awakened. "Yah, why?" she asked, adjusting her window to keep the air from blowing her hair.

"Oh, just daydreaming about my other life. I went to Europe as part of a summer reading program. You know, a chance to get in trouble in my attempt to replicate what I was reading. I did things in

Paris, like making love, for the first time. At that time, all that mattered in life was sex. I had just finished reading Hemingway's *The Garden of Eden.* You know, two broads and one man. Doesn't get any better in life than that."

"Yeah right, jerk. Every woman's dream. By the way, you are a little off geographically. Wasn't the setting for the book in the south of France?" asked Anna.

"Well, okay, I assume you are correct. Can't remember everything. Anyway, it made me remember Paris. Of course, no one can ever forget that city once they have lived it."

"Weren't you a little old for making love for the first time? I assume you were in college. You must have been a real bore on a first date. Hey Steven, have you been to Paris?" asked Anna.

"Well, my story is a little bit more involved so no need to tell it."

"Steven, we have all confessed our sins. It is your turn now," said Anna loudly as she competed with the airstream blowing in from the open windows.

"Well, okay, if it is that important to you. I had a friend with an apartment facing Montmartre. We could see the Basilica of the Sacré-Cœur from the window. He was an artist and a poet. Several steps above our friend Noah. He had a real gift. Of course he was poor, but that didn't seem to matter. Maybe he didn't have a business model," Steven said with a smile.

"When I think of Paris," Noah said, "a quote from John Keats comes to mind: *Give me books, fruit, French wine and fine weather and a little music out of doors, played by someone I do not know.*" Noah continued in his dreamlike trance facilitated by the rhythm of the highway, "I think that pretty well sums up what I think is the perfect evening. Nothing more, nothing less."

"You guys," said Anna, "you are making me want an early meal with your talk of wine and food. Funny how life makes you focus on the basics when you are down and out. When I think of Paris, I think of flirtatious French men, mainly old and overweight ones. The sellers along the Champs-Élysées with their fine car shops, restaurants, and clothing stores. I can still see the blue diamonds for sale in one particular store. They sparkled like a lover's promise. Oh, and then the barge along the Seine at night. Food, music, love − all three on the most romantic of rivers."

Anna too had entered the mesmerizing, hypnotic effect of the swaying bus. "Yes, love was special that evening on the Seine. I was only eighteen and madly in love with a man I had just met. I think he was an author or at least he claimed to be. He even said that one of his books was for sale in Shakespeare and Company. Funny how things happen. You just know it is love. Today I would first do a background check on catchaliar.com."

"Anna, let's just hope that Oracle hasn't been to Paris, too," said Noah.

"What do you mean? Am I talking too much?" questioned Anna.

"Oh no, not at all. You have to admit, you outdid us all with your night in the City of Lights. I only meant that Oracle is the only one who has not admitted to a Parisian affair." Noah looked at the parrot in the rearview mirror.

"Tell us about your night in Paris, Oracle."

"Fuck you! Fuck you! Feed the bird!" said Oracle in his southern accent.

CHAPTER 8

Provincetown

THE ROAD THAT LED TOWARDS CAPE COD WAS FILLED with all types of vehicular traffic. Noah had been warned earlier that the flow of traffic on the highway depended on the hour and day. Even though no one aboard the bus was concerned about it, it happened to be a Friday afternoon.

When it comes to most vehicles, it does not matter to the driver whether the traffic is moving fast or not moving at all, but driving a 1969 bus is different. Nearly every automobile on the clogged artery that day had leather seats that reclined into various positions, air-conditioning, multi-disc CD players, mobile phones, and a panic button for roadway assistance not to mention a GPS. Rocinante had none of these. In addition, its manual transmission required the constant use of the clutch whenever traffic came to a halt.

Unlike Noah, who could with time rebuild every component of his vehicle, the flotsam of New York could not even find their dipstick. Most could not even find the lever that released the lid to their gas cap. Another difference among the drivers and passengers that day, and perhaps most significant of all, no one cared what happened to the occupants of Rocinante.

As arguments and discontent permeated the majority of other drivers and their riders, the isolation of the bus strengthened their bond of friendship very much as if they were outcasts on a rock-strewn beach where no hope of rescue existed.

Noah looked at Anna. "Can you imagine – no food, no cigarettes, no beer, no pot, and no sex all in one day? No one had better ask me what I am giving up for Lent. I have covered enough Lents to last me until the trumpet sounds in the east... or is it the west?"

"Noah, what on earth are you talking about?" Anna asked trying to speak over the wind from the vent window.

"I mean, till I die. Well, no big deal; most of it didn't matter anyway. Sex with no love was meaningless. As far as the rest of it is concerned, we always seem to have food. I don't know how, but we do."

"Noah, you are a con artist, that's how. You conned the farmer's wife into feeding us; you conned Steven and me into your one-act vaudeville show. Honestly, I never thought I would stoop so low. I even considered wearing short shorts. Remember, I was at Sarah Lawrence. I am a trained feminist, and you are definitely the enemy."

"Okay, enemy, you figure out how we are to eat. Are you good at trapping animals? Of course, we have no traps. Perhaps you have a fishhook in your purse."

"There is one thing I excel at and that is making big mistakes in my life. Fortunately for you two has-beens, I am a fairly attractive woman when I want to be. Pull in the next not-so-proper bar and grill, and I will get us a meal."

"Now wait a minute, you are not going to go call girl on us are you?" asked Noah.

"Of course not, I am going to find two men sitting together and plop my fat ass down on the seat next them. Two men always try to outdo one another when it comes to flirting and generosity. I will be bold and ask them to buy me a meal. I will then order the meal that comes with the most food. When I get it, I will eat only a little and ask for a carry-out box. That way my two incompetent friends can have my leftovers," Anna said, looking down the highway for a diner.

"Anna, you are more devious than I am," Noah said, laughing.

Soon Anna spotted her target: STOP AND TALK BAR AND GRILL. "That should do fine. Looking at the not-so-nice cars, I should find men with big hearts in there."

Noah left the highway and downshifted to a stop on the coarse oyster shell parking lot.

"Noah, what is an oyster shell parking lot doing in Cape Cod?" asked Anna. "They must have imported oyster shells from Apalachicola, Florida."

"Hell, man, I don't know a thing about oysters except that I love to eat them raw. You know the taste is not in the oyster but in the sauce. The more bite to the sauce, the better the oyster. You could put the sauce on a cracker, and it would taste just the same," said Steven hungrily from the backseat.

"No way. You haven't eaten an Apalachicola Bay oyster. Nossir," replied Noah. Their conversation was prolonged by their hunger.

"Will one of you has-beens open my door? It's stuck," pleaded Anna. "The least you can do is wish my fat ass luck on my fishing expedition into hell."

"Anna, charm them with your wit or your butt – whichever works best." Steven smiled.

"Is that what I am counting on?" Anna laughed. Both men watched her as she entered the bar.

While waiting, Noah and Steven opened the sliding door and the other hatches of the bus to survive the heat. Eventually, Noah popped the top. A biker who had pulled up near by was having trouble lowering his kickstand. He was middle-aged with a gray ponytail.

"Hey, what are you doing here? It looks to me like we have two faggots in a bus!" shouted the biker. From the tone of his voice and unsteady walk, he was stoned. He was more than anxious to fight someone, anyone. Even the pit stop's dog sensed danger and moved away from the entryway to the bar and grill.

"You wish!" shouted Steven. No more had Steven spoken than Oracle too shouted, "Fuck you! Fuck you! Feed the bird!"

The biker approached the bus. "What the hell did you just say?"

Steven replied, "Sir, he didn't know whom he was addressing. I can assure you that I am not a ventriloquist. The voice you heard was Oracle's. He's a famous show parrot."

"You shitting me?" asked the biker in apparent but now diffused rage. He grabbed the interior of the bus frame and peered in. There behind Steven was Oracle with all of his bright feathers showing.

"I'll be damned, it is a parrot! I want you to know that he just saved your fucking ass. You need to take that bird and shove his fucking throat down the john." The biker then turned away and followed his stomach to the restaurant.

As the minutes passed, Noah said, "Steven, pray for a wind. This sun is cooking my ass. What on earth could be taking Anna so long? Do you think they've hired her as a waitress?"

As soon as he said the words, Anna reappeared walking hurriedly towards the bus. She was carrying sacks of food in both hands. "Crank Rocinante! Normally I don't believe in spurring a horse, but this time I do!"

Noah immediately pressed the pedal hard on the Pepsi bottle and they reentered the congested highway. "What happened in there?" asked Noah.

"Well, I did exactly what I said I would do. Two middle-aged construction workers agreed to buy me a meal. After eating just a little, I asked for a doggy bag. I thanked them and got ready to depart when I saw another carryout sitting on a nearby table. An overweight biker had left it there to go to the john. Well, to make a long story very short, I grabbed it on my way out."

Noah looked at her with a horror-filled expression. "How long do you think it will take the biker to put two and two together and figure out that you got in this bus?"

"Don't worry so much. I could tell he was drinking and probably stoned when he entered the bar. That is why he had to go to the bathroom to vomit his guts out. By the time he figures out where he was seated, we will be long gone provided you can get this thing to go faster. Just to play it safe, I told the two fellows who bought me the meal that I was driving my boyfriend's red Camaro."

The traffic came to a halt on the highway. Then it again began to move very slowly. The roar of a motorcycle approached them on the middle stripe of the two-lane road. It passed them at high speed and continued on towards Provincetown.

"Anna, you can get up from the floorboard now. He just went past us in search of your red Camaro. What did that grisly animal order anyway?" asked Noah.

After digging deeply into the sack, she replied, "You're in luck. Two supersize all-the-way hamburgers with extra fries. One of these could easily feed two of you. By the way, what have you contributed to the meal?"

Noah found his response very limited. "Well, my ability to crank Rocinante in an emergency and get us on the highway despite the fact that I have a red light showing on the gauge. We need to stop again real soon so I can add a quart of oil."

"Will we ever get there?" asked Anna.

"Have you considered the Way of St. James?"

"What the fuck is the professor talking about now?" asked Steven from the backseat.

"My two untraveled compatriots, I am speaking of the Camino de Santiago," said Noah.

Steven sighed. "Next time I am going to hitch a ride with an illiterate person."

Anna remained silent looking out the window at the treeless horizon as the bus sped alongside sand dunes and brackish bays.

"The Camino de Santiago is the route of the pilgrims to the Cathedral of Santiago de Compostela in Galicia. If you make it all the way, you can earn a plenary indulgence from the Church. All sinners, us included, should walk the path. It is done slowly, respectfully, and in a prayerful way."

"What has this got to do with us?" asked Steven.

"Well, you see, we are on a pilgrimage."

"What the fuck, are you comparing Provincetown to Santiago de Compostela? What an imagination! The only thing I can agree with you on is that I am about as uncomfortable, unfed, and thirsty as a medieval pilgrim. When we stop the bus, I want to get my plenary indulgence or whatever it is," said Anna in an unusually serious tone.

"Let's first drive through town and look it over. Then let's find a place to camp. I think there is a state or federal camping site close to the ocean or at least I hope so. Of course, I may have that confused with Providence, Rhode Island."

As the bus entered the congested, narrow Main Street of Provincetown, all of the parking places were taken. It was a town that appeared like its own theatrical production, the stage filled with groups of men and women walking together. Seldom did they see men and women walking as couples. The bars had rows of motorcycles parked in front. Pedestrians frequently walked into the street that soon became a large sidewalk. A few passersby gave them the peace symbol.

Most of the people seemed to gravitate towards a military clothing store for their shopping. Military coats and surplus helmets of every nationality were hot items.

"I don't know what to make of this," said Noah.

"It looks good to me," said Steven with a smile.

"Anna, what do you think?" asked Noah.

Anna laughed. "If I were looking for a man, I don't think I would stop."

"You two are missing the point. I wasn't talking about the sexual orientation of these people, I am asking if you think they might be good customers for us."

Anna responded, "From my point of view, we have the right combination. We have you, the misbegotten poet. We have Steven who is more than able to relate to the audience. Plus, you have me."

"What are you bringing to this event?" Noah asked Anna with a laugh.

"Do you think only men notice a good ass?"

"Okay, I don't think I will ask Oracle. He should fit right in also."

"What I wouldn't give for a drink," said Anna.

"Well, my vagrant friends. You two are in luck. I have three beers and three bottles of Chianti stashed in the back for this moment of conquest. I will even throw in a bag of ice at the campground."

"I will drink it hot." Steven, whose health suddenly seemed to improve, laughed.

"No, Steven, it must be done right, in accordance with the Way of St. James. I insist," said Noah, looking at him in the rearview mirror. "Anna must offer a yoga pose to the Ocean as thanks for our safe journey, and then the cork will be popped and the tabs will be pulled, so say I, Don Quixote."

"Oh no, they charge for parking," said Anna.

"Later on, parking is on me. That is, after the required rituals have been performed. By the way, I have toasted at Saint James's Gate in Dublin, the prestigious home of Sir Guinness's beer," said Steven who suddenly appeared to have some money. "After all, I have played the role of Sancho Panza very well since we met."

The bus soon voyaged towards the end of the earth as it traveled past vacant dunes and sea oats.

"Well, Steven, we will let you pay for a spot on our return when we find the campground. By the way, I'm amazed that you know Don Quixote's squire is named Sancho Panza. I just assumed that you were an ignorant loafer. I now promote you from fool to squire," said Noah as the bus approached the parking attendant who extended an arm and took the money for the camping site. Noah stopped again and dropped some quarters into the ice machine that delivered its five-pound bag of manna to the hot, tired, thirsty occupants of the Ark.

"Noah, park as close to the beach as you can," Anna said, putting her head out the window to look towards the sea. "I love to hear the surf at night. Luckily for us there are several vacant spots available probably due to the heat. The side awning will feel good today."

"Anna, in your quest for shade, you will have to relocate several times due to the many holes in the canvas."

"I guess you are telling me that it has an SPF of zero."

"Not if you move frequently."

"Sancho, help me unload the bus," commanded Noah.

"Are we to call him the Don from now on? What type of trip is he on, anyway? He and I must smoke different weeds," said Steven.

From their campsite, the ocean could be seen between two large dunes. The sun showed brilliantly upon the sand, reflected like precious stones upon the azure blue sea. Above them, the sky was completely clear of clouds as they stopped at the ocean's edge. Close in was a large coastal schooner beating to the northeast, its gleaming white bow splitting the large foam-topped swells.

The earth had abruptly stopped in a swirl of seaweed and small seashells. The occupants felt that they too could step off the end of the earth. The medieval mapmakers were correct in their assumption that the earth was flat; to take a step beyond the edge was to fall.

Down the beach two little girls were playing. Their parents could not be seen. Noah stood looking towards them wondering if he was to be the father of a boy or girl. Would she look like him? At the moment of his greatest triumph, he felt profoundly sad. For a brief moment, not even the sky and sea could console him.

Anna walked up behind him and placed her arm around his waist. "Thank you for this moment." They stood there together looking at the breaking surf without talking further. It was the moment when one kneels before the altar in thankfulness and in silence.

They walked back to the bus. The tops of their feet bright red from the intense sun and the lack of SPF protection. "Well, Don or captain or whatever you are, what's the plan for the evening?" asked Steven.

"The beauty of our new life together is that we have no plan."

"Great leadership, Quixote." Steven laughed.

"As soon as the ice chills the brew, we shall toast our safe arrival at the Cathedral of Santiago de Compostela or at Saint James's Gate, if you prefer. Later at twilight, we will send our faithful Anna in search of a bonfire where men and women drink together and there's meat on the barbie. We will then await her scouting report. If the drinks and food are good and the pot plentiful, we will join them. Perhaps they too are pilgrims at the edge of the earth.

"First, we must perform the ritual of deliverance. Anna, if you will, step forth into the Atlantic and give the lotus pose to Neptune. This looks like a liberal area so you may perform the ritual naturally."

"If I get more sunburned, you will pay the ER bill." Removing her clothes, Anna walked into the surf until the ocean covered her waist. The water felt warm and soothing. She splashed the warm seawater on her shoulders and face. Then solemnly, she saluted the sea god with all due respect.

With her back turned towards Noah and Steven, she appeared like a goddess herself, her beautiful skin reflecting the radiance of the sun. Her wet hair moved to the tempo of the sea as the swells lifted her.

Stephen turned towards Noah. "How could you not love her? She is beautiful even to my eyes."

Noah did not reply yet he felt a sensation of warmth cover his body which had been cooled by the sea breeze. "I do not know how not to love her."

Anna put her clothing back on as Noah and Steven looked seaward. As soon as they entered the protection of the dunes, the heat returned.

Quickly, Noah presented the allotted one beer and one bottle of Chianti to each member of the ark. No gift had ever seemed more appreciated. Anna kissed his cheek.

"Steven, never mind, a handshake will do," she said laughing.

"Not in my book," said Noah as he kissed her cheek in return.

Since they had not eaten for several hours, the alcohol had an immediate effect in that all three fell asleep leaning against each other, their sunburnt feet buried deep in the cool, dust-colored sand.

Noah dreamed he was back on a destroyer stationed in Hong Kong. He remembered his love affair with a Wanchai girl. He had promised to love her only to leave her weeping on Fenwick Pier. He saw the tears streaming down her face as she said, "I afraid you no come back for me." He knew he should have but could not force himself to obey only his heart.

Anna's dream was of her mother and father before the divorce. She saw herself running towards her mother with outstretched arms, her mother turning away from her at the last moment. She then saw her father smiling at her and telling her, "Puddin', it will be okay. It will be okay."

Steven's dream concerned his health. He felt the presence of a person on a black horse waiting to take him to a place where he would be safe. There to be loved; a place in the forest where a mountain stream flowed past talking rocks.

Soon they awoke to a star-filled sky.

"Anna, go do your duty and see if you see any campfires on the beach."

"I must first wash my face. I feel like my eyes are matted too with salt and sand." Anna placed a piece of melting ice into a rag and held it to her forehead. As she walked towards the sea, her feet felt heavy in the sand. Occasionally she would step on the sharp fragment of a shell. She looked in all directions but could not see a campfire. She did not know what time it was for the night was encased in darkness.

When she returned to their dying fire, Anna said, "Sorry, no suckers on the beach tonight. I guess I have failed in my mission to feed us. What kind of sea goddess am I? I can't even find us a hotdog to split."

"Okay, we are no strangers to hunger," Noah said as he struck a mosquito that had landed upon his leg. "Since the insects have discovered us here, let's put our bedrolls near the surf. At least that way, we can catch the sea breeze."

Soon they were stretched out on the beach looking at the stars. Anna reached up for one. "They are so close. I think I can catch a star if I try."

"Anna, how is your book coming along? You have brought new life to my father's typewriter. I often hear you typing late at night."

"Well, okay, I think. Would you mind reading what I have written?"

"No, of course not. It will remind me of my teaching days."

Next morning after her sun salutation sequence, Anna handed Noah a stack of papers. "Here is my life's work, well, this trip's worth, anyway. I would really appreciate it if you would read it. I want you to really be hard on me. If you are not, I will never learn how to write."

"Anna, why are you trying so hard? You and I both know that writing is about winning the lottery. Everyone tries but only a handful, and I mean a handful, actually ever have something published. There is not much opportunity for those of us at the bottom of the rung. First of all, you need a very good and recognized editor. You know, one of those New York types with an upscale address. After you pay them, they will be honest in telling you that you need to start from scratch, that you have no talent and never will have. And to think that you paid them for the insults."

"Okay, so you were disappointed in your attempt at having something published. Maybe I have a story that is a good one. You know, as Hemingway said, there are only a few good stories. I really think mine is worth publishing."

"And what will your story be about? Let me guess, man meets woman and all end's well."

"Do you think I'm that shallow?"

"I am sorry, Anna. You see, I too had a degree of ambition. I think that every English major does, only to find out that you are like every other English major. From the looks of it, I would say that half of Provincetown majored in English and the other half majored in a mixture of art and music. That is why they are here; they are unemployable. Can't build anything, can't repair anything. They, like me, know disillusionment very well. That is why, they, like us, have gathered at the edge of the earth."

"Well, Mr. Goodhope, give my book a try and let me know what you think. You promised me that."

"Anna, so I did. I will keep my word. I will tell you if you are more than a Grade F writer," Noah said as he stuffed the typed manuscript under his seat.

"Noah, please be careful with it. If you lose it, I will feel like Hemingway did when his wife got his manuscript stolen in Paris. I will divorce our relationship. I didn't have any carbons to make a second copy. I can't believe I used the word 'carbon.' What fucking age are we in, anyway? Jeez, living in this bus makes me think it's still the early sixties."

"Okay, tribe, let's try our luck in Provincetown. First, we have to establish a criterion for success. If we make ten dollars above our costs, we have provided a meritorious troop performance worthy of accolades."

Once they had packed their world into the bus, Noah started the bus. The engine roughly tapped into a purr. He got out to check the smoke escaping from the exhaust.

"She is burning pure. Well done, Rocinante."

They entered the highway just as a BMW passed them at high speed. As the car assumed a victorious position in front of them, a young woman stuck her finger up into the air before shifting into a higher gear.

"Fuck you!" shouted Noah out the window. Soon he found a parking meter with time left on it. "Okay, act professional. We must act like we belong here."

True to his word, Steven inserted quarters into the machine. They unpacked the sitar and placed Oracle's covered cage onto the sidewalk. Next, Noah placed his books of poetry on the folding metal stand and connected the speaker. In front of him was the amplifier, making his voice loud enough to be heard above the street noise.

"Dear friends who have searched the world for entertainment, my friends and I have just returned from a European tour. Please forgive my native Irish accent."

Anne and Steven looked at each other with astonishment.

"Let me introduce Seamus from County Galway. He is a renowned sitar player who has played on the streets of Dublin and Paris. You may have read about him in *La Gazette*. He was honored to have performed solo at the Moulin Rouge.

"Next, let me introduce the fair Bridget from County Kerry. Her voice is angelic. She will sing later this evening for you. Today, however, I will be reciting poems that I have shared only in my native city of Dublin. For those fortunate few who purchase my book of poetic travels, I will sign and date each edition sold. Yes, signed and dated. What better memento of your vacation than that of a traveling poet's verse?"

Noah looked at Steven. "Seamus, for the amusement of the children, please unveil our multilingual Egyptian parrot."

Steven leaned close to Noah. "Are you sure about this?"

"Seamus, please unveil our world-famous multilingual conversational parrot."

As soon as the cloth was pulled from the cage, releasing the odor that had been contained within, Oracle spoke loudly to the crowd attracted by the PA system. "Fuck you! Fuck you! Feed the bird."

Unbelievably, the audience laughed. After almost collapsing with laughter, several people stepped forward and placed dollar bills into the container pressed tightly against Anna's hips. In her bewilderment, she had forgotten to pass it around. She too began to laugh.

Luckily for the performing troupe, the police were busy with a drunk that had hit a pedestrian several blocks down the road.

Steven tuned his sitar as the amused crowd awaited more entertainment. Noah remained untouched by the humor of the moment, making the audience laugh even more. Unconcerned, he announced his first poem to be spoken on American soil.

Silence

Silence — a voice stronger than written words.
Does not the text limit that which we think?
Silent words provide direction like the hedge-lined rows of Connemara.

Perhaps my greatest fear, the silence of your words.
Should the voice of a god appear before the unholy crowd?
Consolation derived — for mortal man shall be immortal though bound.

Far worse than bondage in eternal hell.
The darkness without the flame is that most feared.

As he spoke, Anna walked in front of each person seeking an offering. Coins clanged as they struck the bottom of the minnow bucket.

Noah continued with his second composition:

Cast Away

Upon the oceans of the world I have sailed.
Forever a vagabond to that most precious to possess.

Have I not sought you where dreams dwell?
Sandy beach and fiord of the northern realm.

Now I walk the beach alone.
Your memory haunts me still.

My thoughts of you I hurl once more upon the rhythmic swells.
That which is cast into the sea returns to haunt me still.

A young boy asked his father, "Dad, what did he just say?"

"I don't know, but it was good," said the father who was holding a beer and staring at Anna's hips.

The young boy then responded, "Dad, I want to hear the parrot again."

By the end of the day, the parrot had ensured their financial success. Not only had they reached their benchmark of ten dollars, but Noah had managed to autograph seven books of poetry. Knowing that their welcome was only temporary, they collected their stage props and headed back to the campsite but not before they had bought two six-packs of beer and a package of wienies and buns.

Once they finished unloading and were seated on the sand, Anna asked, "How much did we make today?"

"Over a hundred dollars," Noah responded with pride.

"I can't believe it! Your idea actually worked. I even managed to sell a CD of my sitar performance at the ashram in Calcutta. Since I have several CDs in my case, is it alright with you two if I sell them?" asked Steven.

"Just remember that all the money we make will go into the communal pot," replied Noah. "If one succeeds, all succeed. You know, for the first time in my life, I feel successful. To think that dumb bird started our roll of good luck."

"I just want to tell you two that I met two of my former friends today. They are on the city council and have assured me that the police will not harass us. I knew both of them when I was living in San Francisco," said Steven.

"Now that is good news. We will have the summer to get our shit together. Maybe by the end of August, we will know what direction our lives should take. Tonight, Anna, I am going to read your book. Remember, I don't pass out A's to anyone. You will be lucky if I give you a C."

"Hey, professor, I can take the knocks. By the way, thanks," said Anna as she watched seagulls swooping over the dunes on their way to the shoreline.

As the twilight turned to darkness, Noah sat at the folding table in the bus reading the manuscript. The only illumination was a small kerosene lamp that yielded a shadow that danced with the sea breeze.

"Noah, why don't you cut the overhead light on? Are you afraid it will drain the battery?" asked Anna.

"No, I prefer a kerosene lamp when I am reading in the bus. Sort of creates the mood I am looking for."

"Oh, you mean, the vagabond motif?"

"Go do your yoga thing on the beach. I have a lot to read."

That night Anna sat alone on the damp beach sand as the full moon stared at her. The wind was gentle. She closed her eyes and listened to the soft surf that warmed her feet. She thought about Noah sitting there reading her book. She wondered what he was thinking as he turned the pages. "Ah, I can't write. What was I thinking? Just a dream. That is all."

She sat in various meditative poses as the minutes passed. Then she stood up and walked in the moonlight to the bus. Just as she approached, Noah put down his pen where he had been taking notes.

"Well, what do you think? I can't believe you stayed up this late reading it."

"I think they must be teaching young women how to become authors at Sarah Lawrence. I will be truthful, I became so engrossed in your characters that I could not stop reading your work. I don't think I have ever had that problem before, especially with a beginner."

"If it is that good, why have you written down so much criticism?" she said, looking at his notes.

"Do you think the Bible was a first draft? Come on, no one writes a perfect novel just as no one writes a perfect poem. Perfection is up there," he said, pointing towards the Milky Way, "not here."

"Let me see what biting remarks you have written," she said as she began to read his notes.

Noah looked at her. "You don't need to read them. I will tell you. First of all, you have picked a good topic, one that everyone can relate to. You developed your storyline in a logical order. There are a few confusing shifts in time and place. I have marked up the areas that need revision. It would not hurt you to insert more humor into your book. And finally, I would suggest that you get your dialogue to sound more realistic and less stilted. After all, you are writing to entertain, not inform, your reader."

Anna stared at him for a moment. "I don't know how to take criticism even from a friend. It is one of my many weaknesses. Should I just throw it in the dumpster?"

"Well, if you do, I will retrieve it and put my name on it. Well done, Anna."

Anna bent forward over the small table and kissed his forehead. "Thank you, Moses."

.

THE SUN SOON TOUCHED THEIR SKIN. The night had passed too quickly for Anna. She had stayed awake, anxious to talk more about her novel with Noah. She felt very motivated by his comments.

That morning Provincetown was unusually warm. The crowd was larger than it had been the previous day. Their performance continued to amuse the crowd. Every child wanted to hear the talking parrot while their fathers wanted to watch Anna collect the contributions.

After lunch, they separated. Noah watched the bus and their possessions on the street until the other two returned. He preferred to eat a ready-made sandwich while seated in the bus. Since the numbers of visitors had grown, they managed to make over a hundred dollars off book sales and Anna's ability to solicit money from the onlookers, especially parents whose children enjoyed talking to Oracle. It seemed that Oracle had his act together now and was no longer spitting a stream of profanities.

Earlier that morning Noah had noticed Anna talking to a young man. He was very tall with black hair and sunken eyes. About his neck was a thick gold chain with an anchor dangling from it. He was the type that frequented the bars of any beach town. They laughed and talked for a considerable amount of time. Noah was somewhat upset since she had not attempted to seduce others into making a contribution to their act. He had intended to talk to her that evening about her lapse in responsibility.

After Steven returned from lunch at a nearby café, they both waited for Anna. Noah paced up and down the sidewalk peering around the corner of buildings to check if she had walked up an alleyway. After two hours, they disassembled the sitar and other items, carefully loading them back on the bus. Steven asked Phillip, who ran a nearby Army Surplus store, if he would mind Oracle entertaining his customers while they looked for Anna.

Steven and Noah took opposite sides of the street as they walked from shop to shop. They would enter the bars and restaurants and look into the dim light to see if they could see her. Finally they met at Murphy's Bar at the end of the street.

"Steven, I don't know what to think. Anna would never leave us without saying a word. Let's drive to the hospital and see if she has been admitted."

"I talked to a police officer I know, and he has not seen Anna. In addition, he called the hospital for me. She has not been admitted either," said Steven.

"We have no act without her. She is what is generating our source of income among the older crowd. Without her smile and personality no one will contribute a thing. I can't believe that she would vanish just as we have gotten our act together. That is just not like her," said Noah as he sipped a Guinness.

"I don't know what to do. I checked the parking lots alongside the pier, and there is no Anna. I looked into parked cars, and she was not there. I even talked to Molly at The Black Earring where she nearly always eats lunch, and she said that Anna never showed up," Steven said, continuing to look around the bar as though expecting her to magically appear.

"This bothers me. We care about each other too much for her to just wander off without a word. Let's look a few more hours, and then report her as missing," said Noah, his concern showing in both his mannerism and voice.

"Noah, you can't report a missing adult without proof of an abduction. Adults have a right to just wander off. Nearly one hundred percent of the time they show up later drunk, stoned, or with another lover. I can understand why the police do not look for them."

That evening, Noah and Steven drove back to the campsite. Neither of them wanted to speak to the other. They sat there in the twilight consumed in their thoughts. Then Noah spoke. "What was I thinking of? I was falling in love with Anna. I should have known that it would not work out for me. I still remember her talking to a fellow with long black hair. If I can spot a drug user, and I should be able to, he was one. Tattoos, cigarettes, and no shirt. What an asshole. Well, I guess he wasn't as bad off as I thought since I am the real loser," said Noah in a voice filled with emotion.

"Noah, you can't control everything. If she wants to, she will come back. Just be patient," said Steven.

The next morning they did not leave early for Provincetown. Steven had slept later than he normally did.

"Steven, Steven, wake up man. It is time for us to fry some baloney. I have already made coffee."

"Noah, I don't feel well. As you know, I have been a pretty sick fellow for a long time. I haven't been taking my medicine as I should. I want to show you something." Steven rolled up both his sleeves and his pant legs, something he never did in the sunlight.

Noah just assumed that since he was very thin, he just did not feel the uncomfortable heat that others did.

"My god, Steven, what are those sores? I can't believe you didn't mention this me. I would have taken you immediately to a hospital."

"Dude, I am dying. I don't want to be afraid or to hurt anymore. I want it to be quick."

"Come on, what are you talking about? They have all kinds of drugs for AIDS. Don't be such a horse's ass. Let's get you to a doctor."

"Just like any type of disease, some can take the medicine and others cannot. I was never very lucky," said Steven.

At that point, Noah felt his own tears running down his cheeks. He grabbed Steven and hugged him to his breast. "No, man, no! You can't do that to me. What will Anna think of you if you are not a fighter? You have a reputation to protect. After all, how many sitar players are willing to play for a loser like me? You capture the feelings of my poems in your music."

"You are a good man, Noah. Who else would have taken me in but you? You have to let me go. No matter how much it hurts, you have to let me go."

Noah's tears fell upon Steven as he lifted him. "I am taking you to the hospital right now. We are going to get you shipshape. No one dies on my watch! You hear that, man?"

Noah drove immediately to the local hospital where, after completing several forms, Steven was admitted. Noah sat in the waiting room looking out onto the street. He could not imagine his life now without Steven and Anna.

As he sat in the waiting room, the police officer that Steven knew came into the waiting room. "I thought you might be here," said Officer Zenanko. "Steven told me he was feeling pretty damn bad. It was only a matter of time until he would need palliative care. Damn, this disease has killed so many of my friends." They stared at each other for just a moment. "Noah, there is something else I have to tell you. Your friend, Anna, is in jail. Her old boyfriend from Charleston was cooking meth in a beach house. We raided it and found them both inside."

Noah sat stunned by the news. He only looked at the officer, unable to form any words.

"There was no proof that Anna was involved in the manufacture and distribution of an illegal substance. The judge will be lenient on her, I think. Steven knew about it but did not want to tell you. He is the one who talked to her court-appointed attorney about a reduced charge."

"What reduced charge?" asked Noah.

"Well, I imagine that it will only be possession and use. I think that is what it will be. Now about that loser who was with her, the judge is going to throw the book at him. Drugs make their way into Provincetown, but we don't need the reputation of manufacturing them here. Can you imagine if parents of teenagers found out we were the meth capital of Massachusetts?"

Noah looked into the eyes of the policeman. "Did she mention me?"

"No, sir, I only made the connection through Steven. He said that you had kind of fallen for her. Lucky for you, you didn't fall head-over-heels in love with her. When we found her, she was naked on the floor lying in her own excrement. What a sight." The officer continued, "You know most of those who are doing meth never come back to the normal side of things. It just changes them. The only positive thing about Anna is that she doesn't look like a meth head.

Usually, their teeth are rotten, and they look much older than their real age. She must not have been a fulltime user of that poison."

"When will she be released?" asked Noah.

"Real soon, I guess, but someone will have to sign for her. Someone the judge can trust to take care of her and get her into rehab."

Noah looked once more into the officer's eyes. "What about Steven? How long does he have?"

"Not long. He didn't want to live until he met you two. I think you both were the only good thing that ever happened to him. By the time he wanted to get well, it was too late. Pneumonia often kills people like Steven very quickly. I am really sorry. I know he is your friend, too."

Noah rose from his chair and approached a nurse. "My friend Steven is in room 406. When I first got here, they said no visitors. That was several hours ago. Might I step in and see him?"

"I will check for you." She stepped inside the central nursing station desk and made a call. "I see, okay thanks." The nurse nodded. "Sir, you may go up for just a minute. They don't want him to have any lengthy visits."

"How is he doing?" Noah asked reluctantly.

"Oh, they have not fully informed you, have they? Mr. Myers is very ill. He is developing signs of late AIDS progression. He has developed pneumonia. I understand that you are his friend. I don't know how he kept this from you."

"I guess I never really wanted to know the truth."

Noah followed the nurse's instructions on how to reach room 406. He gently knocked on the door. As he opened it, he could hear Steven's labored breathing.

"What the fuck are you doing here?" Noah asked fully knowing the truth.

"Oh man, it just happens. Give Oracle to Molly at the bar. She will take care of him. He should fit right in there with her customers. The only thing I have left is the sitar. Take it and pawn it. Since it is handmade and unique, don't take less than five hundred for it. You get me?"

"Steven, let's get you well, and then we will talk about Oracle and your worthless sitar."

"Noah, promise me one more thing: take care of Anna. She needs you."

"Steven, now wait a minute, she doesn't give a shit about me. You…" Noah stopped talking for Steven was no longer looking at him. Suddenly, his monitoring machine sounded a flat-line alarm.

"Nurse, nurse!" shouted Noah.

CHAPTER 9

Letting Go of Dreams

Noah sat alone with his feet buried in the sands of Cape Cod. The coolness of the sand felt very good. Only five people had attended Steven's funeral, each one in cutoffs and sandals. Noah alone cried during the short, rehearsed, and too frequently given sermon. Steven was buried among other destitutes in the most simple of graves.

After the funeral, Noah had returned to the campsite. At first, he just sat in the heat, sweat rolling down his cheeks mixing with the tears from his eyes. His world had once more collapsed around him.

As he sat there with his hands resting upon the sand, Officer Zenanko pulled up behind him.

"I am glad I found you. Steven said this is where you three were camped. Anna asked me to see you. Do you want to sign for her or not? Believe you me, I would suggest really thinking about this before making a decision. Sometimes what seems simple can become highly complex. Personally, I think that you will be crazy if you do."

"How do I get to the jail?" asked Noah.

"Just follow me. I will take you there."

As he drove, Noah remembered Anna bathing in the ocean, their late night talks, and the kiss on the Ferris wheel high in the sky. He also remembered her flirting with the stranger who took her from him. For every reason to sign for her, there were ten reasons not to. As last he concluded, "I have lost Steven. How can I also lose Anna though wounded she be? I have no one else but her."

He parked in the assigned parking lot and entered the jail. There he met the court-appointed attorney.

"Mr. O'Brien, my name is Murlis Edwards. I am legal counsel for Anna Lemrick. I understand from Anna that you are willing to sign for her and to assure the court that she will seek help in her drug addiction. She was originally charged with a felony, but your friend Steven appeared before the judge in order to have the charge reduced to a misdemeanor. I personally think that she should have been charged with felony possession and possibly prostitution but then it was not up to me. I guess the Good Lord intends everyone to have a second chance."

"Steven was a good man. There are very few of them. He was always protecting us even when we did not know it," said Noah.

"I don't think you really know how good he was. In his will, he left his estate to both of you. Not that there was that much money, but enough to carry you over for a while," said Murlis.

"Can I see Anna now?" asked Noah.

"She is being processed and should be here shortly," said the attorney.

When Anna walked through the door, Noah's heart broke. Her eyes were sunken and red from crying and lack of sleep. Her arms were bruised, and she was shaking. Her lips were also bruised and cut.

"Anna, will you come with me?" asked Noah.

"Oh, it's Noah, and he wants me to board his ark. I guess I will be your crewmember since I don't see any more offers on the horizon. Where is Steven?" she asked.

"You don't know?" replied Noah. "He is dead." Upon hearing the news, she collapsed to the floor, crying. "Anna, Anna, it's okay. Steven is not suffering now. It will be okay." He lifted her from the floor and embraced her tightly. "Steven left us enough money so we can eat something and get you well."

"Noah, how come you are always there to pick up the pieces of other people's lives? Now that Steven is dead, who will pick you up?" she said looking him in the eyes.

"I don't know, I really don't know," replied Noah.

CHAPTER 10

Recovery and Departure

WEEKS PASSED QUICKLY ON THE BEACH. Each day Anna grew stronger and each day Noah loved her more. It was as though the earth had reappeared above the floodwaters.

"Noah, I have been using Molly's address to receive mail. Guess what? Today a package arrived from a publisher in New York City. I didn't want to open it until I was with you."

"Anna, let me see it. I have never received good news from a publisher. If it is a rejection, it is the thickest one that has ever been sent. No, you open it. It is your story."

Anna's hands were trembling as she ripped open the oversized envelope. Her face lite up immediate as she jumped up. "Noah, Noah, they want to publish it! Enclosed is a check for one hundred thousand dollars!"

"Come on, Anna, be serious. Our kind never wins. Read on. There are probably strings attached just like with those condominium salesmen and their offers of a free vacation."

"Well, prophet, feast your eyes on this one."

Noah's hands took the check, and then he stared at it. "I can't believe my eyes. Is this for real?"

"Yes, it is for real. That damn manual typewriter, and you made this happen. All that editing you did for me and the suggestions, my lord, the suggestions. It all came together!"

That night neither Noah nor Anna talked. They looked at the moon once more rising over the Atlantic. "Look, Noah, you remember the shooting star on the Ferris wheel? There it is again. I know it is the same one." Anna continued, "Tomorrow I am going to deposit that check. Yes, I can't wait to see their banking eyes when they look at it. I am already thinking of more books, more plots. I have finally made it just like my Sarah Lawrence professor said I would!"

Noah looked at her and wondered what would become of Anna. He knew that just as meth had controlled her body, fame would now control her life. "Anna, when you gain something, you always lose something – that is what my grandmother said. Perhaps it is true."

"Oh, come on, Noah, no room for a pessimist anymore. I can write! I can write!"

"As you climb to the top and I have no doubt you will, just remember the three of us."

"What do you mean, remember? You are coming with me. Only a chicken shit would say no. Besides you're good-looking. You could function as my window dressing."

"Truly, Anna, what would you want me for? I don't think you will be living in a bus anymore nor will you need a driver of a manual shift vehicle."

"Suit yourself, Noah. I am in no mood to argue with you. You can at least tell me you love me."

"Anna, I have loved you from the first moment I saw you."

CHAPTER 11

A Moment in the Sand

IN THE LATE TWILIGHT, WHILE SEATED ONCE MORE around the campfire, Anna rose and took Noah's hand. "I think that this is a good evening for us to swim together. The moon has just risen above the sea and the breeze is gentle."

Noah did not speak as he rose. He felt the warmth of her hand as they walked on the still warm sand. With each step, the sand felt good between their toes.

Upon reaching the wet sandy beach where the waves barely touched the earth, Anna undressed until she was wearing only a garment of moonlight. Noah undressed as well, and then holding hands they entered the warm sea. Beams of the moon penetrated the crests of the waves that swept towards them.

Anna stopped and looked into Noah's eyes. He took her hand and placed it upon his chest. They embraced as their lips found one another.

Together they walked to the shore. There in the shallows, with the water just touching her shoulders, the warmth of her body engulfed his own. Their hips moved like the waves that gently touched their bodies. Their passion within uniting them.

Exhausted, they turned on their backs and looked at the stars as they had so often done on their trip. "Noah, why didn't we make love before? I know what you said earlier about wanting to be sure that you did not hurt anyone else, but that was just an excuse. Think of all the pleasure that we could have had together. By the way, you are a great lover. I have never before felt such fulfillment in sex."

Noah was silent as he watched a meteor shoot across the sky. "Anna, did you see the shooting star? We too have only a moment of perfection. The beauty of a moment does not last. I love you, that is true. How could any man not be in love with you or fail to want to have you? There is such a restless need in me to find what I am looking for, and you are the same way. We could search together, I know, but our search will lead us to different directions."

THE NEXT MORNING NOAH LEFT ANNA AT THE BANK to deposit her check. He visited Molly and the others who had been so good to the tribe. He then went back to The Black Earring where they were to meet. Two hours passed as he drank beer and waited for Anna. Finally, he left and walked to the bank.

"Excuse me, may I help you?" asked the young teller who greeted him with a smile.

"A young woman came in two or three hours ago and made a substantial deposit. She had blond hair and was wearing a denim skirt with a blue blouse."

"Oh, how could I forget her? Not many people come in and make such a large deposit. She said she was going to fedex some papers to the Big Apple."

"Where did she go?"

"The FedEx office at the end of the block."

Noah walked to the office and entered the air-conditioned interior. "Excuse me, but a young woman came in earlier and sent some documents to New York. Did she say where she was going?"

The agent replied, "She asked if she could use my personal computer. It seems like she was trying to book a flight. Then she asked me where to get a taxi to the local airport here in Provincetown."

"Where was she going?" he repeated the question.

"She did not say. I am sorry," replied the staff member. "If your name is Noah, she left this for you. She said that you would be looking for her."

After taking the letter, he opened it. It contained a note and a check for $10,000.

My Love:

You were right, it could not have worked out. I will never forget you, Steven and, oh yes, Oracle. You saved me that rainy night in South Carolina and had faith in me. Perhaps we will meet again on some distant highway or at another beach. At every truck stop, just look for a woman in shorts with nothing to lose. It will be me.

With all my love,
Anna

CHAPTER 12

The Speech

It was not long before Anna's speech to over a thousand would-be authors, agents, and publishers was to be given. As she walked up to the podium, the audience responded with applause. Her journey had not been as she had planned. Perhaps it was the unexpected in her life that had given her the greatest gift of all.

As always, she opened her remarks by saying, "First of all, I want to thank Noah and the other passengers in the Ark." She looked towards the back of the audience where a tall, lean man stood alongside a beautiful young woman who looked very much like him. He held a musical instrument case in one hand. Then she remembered the line from Noah's poem: "That which is cast into the sea returns to haunt me still."

Poetic Moments

INSPIRATION
FROM THE IMPRESSIONISTS

Friends and Lovers

Friends and lovers,
Upon the lawn they meet
To share the harvest fruit with wine and honey sweet.

The sun embraces each within the day.
Yet an umbrella foretells the changing fortunes of the sky.
The trees will soon bend with swirling wind.

Clothes of position stately worn for status is a sacred art.
No peasant the feast shall share.
Field mice the crumbs will bear to humble nests within the glen.

Let us make haste while we are immersed in sunlight's warmth.
Tarry not within ourselves or be divided in our love.
No stranger will drink the wine nor taste the honey upon the bread.

It is a moment that we alone shall share.
Is not love a selfish act between two friends?
Passion consumed like wood within the flame.

The day will end with thunder's clap.
Then walk with me in falling rain.
My voice, assurance gives, that affection will last as twilight fades.

My love not hidden by darkening clouds or veils of mist.
It will speak within the night when we as lovers meet.
To be resurrected like wind-tossed meadows in morning light.

Water Lilies

I flee from where I dwell.
No longer content with whom I am.
A victim of myself alone in sunlit fields.

Upon the pond, reflections live.
A palette of colors revealed.
Hues of the sky and field prevail.

Pastels meet to swirl with windblown breath.
A dragonfly flies forth upon wings of silk.
The warmth of the sun now paints upon my thoughts.

Are you here, my love, to hear my song?
To smell the flowers that frame the pond.
Now fall asleep upon my breast where the heart does dwell.

Starry Night Over the Rhone
Vincent Van Gogh (1888)
Musée d'Orsay, Paris

The Descent of Stars

In Paris the stars descend from the sky.
Upon the river they dwell to tempt the weak,
The moon having fled the realm of gods.

The scent of wine and freshly baked baguette.
The call of Montmartre is in the air.
Can I resist when stars touch the earth within the night?

Beneath a manmade light she waits for me.
My faith to be cast upon the street.
It is not the Basilica of the Sacré-Cœur I seek.

It is not safe when stars float upon the Seine.
Inhibitions chastened by wine and mocked by man.
Upon the streets of Montmartre she weaves her web.

How long can I resist such a scene?
Cast from Eden's gate to dwell with needs unmet.
A pilgrim who desired faith, but sought a courtesan instead.

The Boulevard

I walk upon a boulevard of strangers.
Cars play their horns upon the street.
Wants displayed within the shops to tempt me.

The aromas of tobacco and leather-bound books within a shop.
The scent of breads and black forest mousse.
The breath of a cabaret entices me to enter within.

What is it that I desire this winter day?
Can it be purchased in a boutique?
Perhaps it is food and wine I seek.

The soul searches within.
No street or shop provides me with what I seek.
Perhaps in candlelight it is revealed.

A hill known by artists
From Claude Monet to Henri de Toulouse-Lautrec.
Within Montmartre dwells
The Moulin Rouge and the Basilica of the Sacré-Cœur.
A choice to be made between the soul and desires of man.

Wheatfield with Crows
Vincent Van Gogh (1890)
Van Gogh Museum, Amsterdam

Wheatfields of Saint-Rémy-de-Provence

Colors harvested among the fields of wheat.
Yellow turns to brown at harvest season.
Crop of winter green; gold of the summer sun.

Crows and others join the feast at harvest time.
Field mice nourished upon the earthen table.
Crickets performing to the anointed moon.

The lane before me travels to the sky.
Followers of the earth and keepers of the hoe,
All tread upon the winding road.

Before me fields of abundance lay.
Yet within me hunger plays the fiddle loud.
I am not fed by bread alone.

The nourishment that I seek is within your smile
Unreachable as the summer sky,
The end of a lane within a field of wheat.

Dance at Le Moulin de la Galette
Pierre-August Renoir (1876)
Musée d'Orsay

Jovial Encounter

Your youthful smile reaches forth to tease.
Can I deny the grasp of your eyes upon my emotion?
Lips that speak not the truth, but the falsehood of desire.

The music shouts as lovers cling about the room.
Cigarettes enhance the mood of painted thought.
A blend of absinthe and cognac mixed within a glass.

Am I not lost within the gaiety of others,
To laugh with words unheard?
Social graces redefined within Le Moulin de la Galette.

I am here to wear the masks of others.
Shared roles played to mutual laughter.
Pretenders of love who mix desire with self-doubt.

Reefs of the sea with intent less clear,
Should not I have left for lands of rocky cliffs
To wash myself in the purity of a Celtic rain?

A victim of absinthe and cognac,
Unable to flee the grasp of your stare.
A voice unheard amidst the jovial laugh of others.

POEMS
AND OTHER THOUGHTS

A Whisper

Hope should shout but it speaks in whispers.
How could that which sustains remain so silent in the night?

In wind-tossed fields of wheat there is a whisper.
To pray to that unseen except in shades of summer green.

Hope is a prayer gently spoken in the night.
Yet unheard though by my side you contently sleep.

Let not truth or reason speak.
Harsh reality has no place within a lover's heart.
It is that unspoken now heard.

To seek the solace of the unseen is my desire.
Beside the gentle brook in thought alone to dwell.
To reside in quietness without fear.

Three Parts Divided

A beach of sand and rock,
A still lagoon protected from the rising swell.
A sky with clouds that drift above.

Divisions clearly seen.
Can we discern a thought so clear?
Upon a beach where dreams both flow and ebb.

Division before me divided into three equal parts.
Is not the godhead so?
We are the beach, the sea and sky.

Not so the complexity of our lives.
Images mixed and stirred by fate,
Alone do mingle without a thought.

I would that life could be so clear.
The past, present and future shown pure.

A trinity of ideas clearly painted upon the easel.
Divisions recorded within words.

Too Late the Dawn

Can my life awaken like the dawn?
Renewed the sounds of meadows and twilight-touched glades.
The moon hung but for a moment in a sycamore tree.

Have I slept too late to see the rays of light upon the pond?
The movement of awakened bees.
Fireflies now flee to the darkness of the shade.

Warm Shallow Sea

With the morning tide,
I stroll upon seashells and frothy foam.
Alone the coffee sits cold upon the sun-drenched tabletop.

It is the moon I seek, not the sun,
With blinding light and shadows formed.
Uninvited thoughts have beckoned me.

Does not the ocean roar at dawn?
To sleep most gentle,
 When constellations stroll about the dome?

Oh dream of peace sough within.
Where can I go when the sunrises,
As shadows form within?

Seeking That Which Cannot Be Found

Do we not all seek that which cannot be found?
The finest wine, the sweetest lips satisfy not
The thirst within the soul.

I have sought thee in foreign lands.
Upon Knocknarea I have stood before the ancient queen.

Barren dream of contentment sought.
It shall elude us all till the end.

The Wisdom of Age

The wisdom of age is not to be found in book or merry song.
It is but one act played upon a stage.
An illusion created to amuse an audience of friends.

In youth I sought to know it all.
The wine of thought freely poured.
Empathy remained a stranger without.

Am I content to sit and wait for the dark shadow and chilly cold?
Inevitability awaits the dealing of the cards.
Let my thoughts play in the warm meadow sun.

It is now that I have sought.
Content to love and be loved,
Embraced within your arms.

My Beautiful One

The meadow is clothed in morning mist,
Yet the lark sings.

You lie beside me in slumber soft.
Your form revealed by awakening light.

I must touch you now.
To awaken you as sunlight streaks the dawn.

There is no time to waste asleep.
We must talk while time remains.

Beautiful form asleep before me now.
Awaken to the touch of words.

Touched by You in Morning Light

Your smile adorns the awakening light.
Scents of honeysuckle and gardenia drift within the garden wall.

Birds dart to one another above the wooden fence.
Falling water plays softly as it cascades upon keys of stone.

Memories hover about the stream.
Soft mist rises to greet the dawn.

Upon you the light falls in gentle strokes.
The cat purrs and then reclines at your feet.

Bees stir the flowers' scent.
Love experienced in the silence of a thought.

Only the present resides in such a moment of delight.
Touched by you in the golden light.

To Desperately Seek You

How does one seek that which cannot be found,
In dim light or in the comfort of a voice?

Am I awake or intoxicated by slumber,
An apostle to a dream.

Can I call aloud to you who exist only within a thought?
Names are but voices in desolate places.

Shattered like glass upon the floor I lie.
Fragments do not remake the whole.

Afraid alone, alone afraid, an interplay of words now heard.
That which seeks to stir me from a dream unseen.

Awakening but lengthens the day not sought,
To feel the dagger deepen within my heart.

I desperately seek you where hope has fled.
To smile once more, sleep renewed if only for a moment.

A pauper yet wealth abounds.
Return, my love, embrace me
If only a touch be allowed.

Pin Oak Park

Like painted figures in the Moulin de la Galette
They sit in silence yet smiles abound.
The music plays but is not heard.

For whom do they wait?
Strangers and friends are but one.
Do not all laugh or frown in the unison of a crowd?

The Woman with the Long Blond Hair

In the sidewalk café, red wine is sipped.
The gazette flung carelessly upon the bench.
A cigarette, with growing black ash,
Rests obediently between forefinger and thumb.

A solitary day to spend beside the Seine.
Painted clouds dry in the warm wind.
Pigeons seek bread from beneath the tabletop.

Suddenly she appears.
The woman with the long blond hair.
A dream that walks alone.

She stands but for a moment to toss her hair once more.
Motionless she gazes upon the waters of the Seine.
I can no more than look upon her form.

Like the model from a painter's art
She stares at water, trees and clouds painted by light.
Our eyes never meet yet I long for her.
The woman with the long blond hair.

The Hillside

Upon the hillside gathering mushrooms
And wild herbs under the Umbrian sun.
A still image of my desire is painted within my thought.

Create words for me that I might see you there.
Green leaves and mountain flowers softly caressed
By wind that moves your hair and summer dress.

The sun lightly rests upon your shoulders.
The breath of flowers fill the restless air.
The sound of rushing streams transforms the weariness within.

How can words upon a page speak your voice?
Can that unseen be loved?
Strangers do not share the thirst of such desire.

I shall not be content to read images upon a page.
Words do not the emotions form.
It is only a silhouette that I now see.
Complete the image that I might dwell within.

Though our lips embrace in silence.
The longing within my heart fulfilled upon a summer hill.
A lady gathering mushrooms and wild herbs.

Lips of pictorial youth frozen by the artist's hand.
Their love, a silent fresco, alone remains.

A Room of Shadows

Within dark passages they dwell.
That which blocks the light creates its own desire.

Dependent on the sun and burning flames.
Shadows do not speak yet words are formed.

As they dance before the flame,
That which creates the shadow masks the light upon the wall.

Only that which exist can the shadow form.
Voiceless silhouettes that pantomime pretensions within.

Actors that play the jester's part
Mimic life upon the stage.

A shadow play of handheld marionettes
Strings do control us all played by forces unseen.

I exist within a land of shadows.
In tones of gray I dwell.
In the Book of Kells only black and white are written.

A silhouette of others I remain,
Yet my desire for you is real.

I am aflame for you within.
A shadow created by the image of your form.

Invitation

Who sits at my table though unseen?
Have I sought thee from the past when gods ruled the summer sky?

The wind from off the glade speaks, and I hear your voice.
'Tis my folly I know to be joined by that which cannot be.

Do not dreams dwell within us all?
A visitor unseen that sits within my presence.

The formless guest who consumes my vintage wine
And laughs with me.
A pretender of the real as my friend.

Has longing joined me so freely?
Where are you that I might touch?
My soul speaks to you aloud in voiceless words.

My Beloved

The river journeys past the needs of my life
As the sun sets the sea aflame.
The moving waters of my soul flow to you.

My life compiled within a ledger of promises to keep.
If I can but recall them all, while some I cast beyond my reach.

Loneliness commands the obligations within my grasp.
To wake with you beside a gentle sea is all that I ask.

Within your arms, time will cease.
You are my beloved.

Where I Choose to Dwell

I dwell upon the shear granite mountains
That face the roaming waves of Dingle.
The sound of rushing water
Falling from cliffs of stone carved by nature's anger.
Yet within, the definition of myself looks seaward
Towards a new sun's arrival.

Yew, oak and mountain pine.
The garment threads upon which I cling.
Sweet fragrances of the mountain air
Infiltrate the glistening glens below.

A bed of many quilts I lie upon, while a fire warms the room.
A storm of rain upon the roof plays its part in harmonious note.
How long to dream until the sun casts the sea with flame.

A touch no more than a whisper.
Your presence is there with me like a river's mist.
I am a part of you.
It is to my lover that I rush with impatient haste.

Is the warm sea a better place to be?
A drink upon a porch of thatch.
The rhythm of the Pacific swells to match my quickening pulse.

Perhaps a Tuscan sun to lure me to your side.
A decanter of wine to accompany you and me.
Helios to kiss your arms, legs and lips upon a Roman beach.

A shell to gather and discard while waves upon the reef are cast.
Lovers unclothed upon a beach.
The sun too soon marks its place upon our skin.
The moving waters of my soul flow to you.

We speak in foreign languages to one another.
We pause in communal thoughts beneath our separate suns.
My wish, to taste the wine upon your lips.
To linger in your smile within a night
Obedient to desire alone.

Waiting for the Flight

Like all that I see before me,
Too long the delay in life's mad dash.
Impatient for the hour of planned departure.
We wait in haste for indifference to occur.

Among those that do not speak.
Conversations heard on cell phones with text,
Void of feeling.
A collection of strangers to intimacy.

To ease the pain of my diet,
A beer, grilled sub and fries.
Perhaps a Kindle to connect to the past.
Towards a city of discontent I fly today.

It is upon a sea of air that I will ride.
The carpet is smooth and clouds are far below.
An aisle sea preferred; seat c-b-a or f-e-d I cannot recall.

We race to meet another,
To interrupt their lives but for a moment.
Boarding pass too soon to print before the dawn.

Eyes do not connect while waiting.
A Coke, Pepsi, and coffee.
The complimentary drinks of the frequent flyer.

Pilots who look more old and tired than I,
Stare upon the floor as they pass by.
A journey into the celestial sky.
The return to where we left
Is more desired than the journey among the stars.

Desire is a glance to steal.
My identity a barcode upon paper.
Did my luggage really weigh that much?
Will you be there upon my arrival?

The Dweller of the Forest

What is reality but a thought?
Age is but youth disguised.

Within the forest we dwell together
Dreamers of a summer night.

With words we share the evening's touch.
Let us press gently upon the other's heart.

The night is alive with the stars and moonlit clouds.
Let us share our vision though apart in other worlds.

To stare together at the rising moon.
Apart and yet as one;
Let us sleep not alone within the night.

A Thousand Years

Have I known you a thousand years?
A vision that before me now appears.

As vines that within the forest interweave;
Passion found within a dream.

Beside the fountains of the earth we dwelt.
In haunted nights we meet to touch.

Love fulfilled beneath the pagan moon.
A thousand years have passed, and now we meet anew.

I dwell in fitful slumber.
Dreams appear in the chamber of the night.

Afraid of that which appears before me now,
A bondservant obedient to a vision.

Emotions of the night are words that speak within the soul,
To comfort and to tease the dreamer.

A vivid impulse among strangers seen.
Images of the past appear to haunt my slumber.

How does one love and not an offering make?
Can a gift of words within a dream complete the journey?

Too soon awakened in the light of subdued colors,
Yet the image of the dream remains.

My Lover of Words

Is there an answer for who a person really is?
Celtic heritage, professor or friend.

Regardless of the success and failure of my life,
I see the measurable ending of the light.

I am too realistic to believe that answers can be found.
Only questions abound within the night.

A moment to feel beside a fountain alive with water and sunlight.
All that I am seeking now.

I know that contentment is not a constant companion,
Only moments are allowed.

Please permit me the foolishness of one shared thought with you.
The most beautiful moment that exists is within a verse.

The Gods Do Play

Upon Olympus they recline,
Safe in their celestial realm.

Below the saint and sinner search for love.
When found there is only sound and fury.

How brief the moments of our love.
Soon the flame shall vanish into the darkness.

The smoke lingers but for a moment.
The gods do play with us to their delight.

To the One That Knows

Lie with me upon the summer meadow,
Like words entwined within a verse.

Upon your breast I lie contented,
To hear the heartbeat within my lover.

Can we stay but an hour?
Soon the winds of fall will appear.
The warm moonlight turned to chilling frost.

Yet within this moment two lovers,
Entwined like words within a verse.

The Beach

The warmth of the sun comforts you.
Skin cleansed by the salty sea.

Among crowds you smile and are content.
Along the beach the dachshunds play.

Let not your thoughts return to Rome.
Sip the wine and do not think of me.

A visitor of dreams within the night.
A friend in shadows to caress and forget.

The warm beach shall be your friend and lover.
Sun and sea now touch your lips and lay with you upon the sand.

To Be Gentle

Let us be gentle with our hearts.
There is much to learn of one another.

Life has taken us to strange places.
Angry seas and wind-struck mountains.

Apart we dwell in worlds unknown to the other.
Yet seeking to love and be loved of a stranger.

The Visual Part of Man

Does man vanish like a vision upon a glass?
A moment of time to play a part,
Then the silence of the stage.

Do we see in all dimensions or understand all things?
Adrift upon a world that is tethered to a star,
We marvel at the light.
There are few answers revealed
Till time itself shall cease within the void.

There are no natural laws that order our desire.
The human heart is not ruled by the logic of man.
Desire the rule itself dictates.

We are the icebergs of the northern sea.
The visual part alone we understand.
Seek not that which others see.
Hidden from view is the soul of man.

Thoughts upon a Mediterranean Beach

Beneath the sun let us shout our joy.
Should we not touch our lips to wine and laughter?

Each moment to salute.
Alive beneath the Italian blue sky.
A joy to discover who we are.

Helios alone will kiss thy lips.
Love renewed under the Mediterranean sun.
Embraced by the sea,
Till twilight fades and Pegasus returns.

Constellations

Placed within the sky to never touch.
Companions to Helios and Diana.
To rule the night yet alone.

Lovers see the star-filled heavens,
Immortal flames of the night.
But not the hurt that dwells within.

Does purity alone reside within their heart?
Can we approach and please the gods,
Or is isolation the command?

Forever beautiful in a field of stars.
To please the gods to remain untouched.
Does natural law permit so harsh a rule?

Should stars a comet form?
To flame across the darkened sky,
To be cast into the sea together?

A destiny to become the dust of other worlds.
Infants within the void of time to remain in pursuit.
A view for lovers upon a beach who see the trail of flaming stars.

A beautiful glow above the sea is formed.
Their sorrow shared by mortal man.
Seen by lovers who are afraid to touch yet pursue.

Ostia Antica

What among the stone remains of ancient songs and fervent games?
Conversations of the wind alone are heard.

A lover's whisper is the breeze.
The shout of the crowd in thunder's roar.

Now birds speak aloud among the ruins.
They walk upon the mosaic images of forgotten gods.

The sweet fragrance of the cypress lingers in the air.
The sun nests within the topiary-shaped trees.

Lovers revealed in secret places upon the stone.
Frescoes of another age perform their plays beneath the trees.

I to the Mediterranean will flee while the sun warms the sea.
To drink sweet absinthe; then ancient songs will appear.

Toward Ostia Antica I glance.
The drum of pagan dance and song are heard.

Lips of pictorial youth frozen by the artist hand.
Their love, a silent fresco, alone remains.

A Letter to the Poetessa of Rome

Words of verse are spoken across the seas.
Only poetry reads the soul and speaks the lover's voice.
To a dream they pursue and speak.

Have I known you before when we walked beneath the Tuscan sun?
A time of festivals and earthen-toned wine.

Upon a deserted beach we walked
When Jupiter over Olympus reigned.
Stars spewed forth into immortal constellations
That rule the darkness of the night sky.

I have searched for you in the piazzas of Rome.
I have climbed the Spanish Steps and called your name.

Words that speak aloud in song and verse.
In flight they travel to the heart unseen.

Within the courtyard of another land I write to you.
In sunlight nourished yet my soul in lonely pursuit remains.

The clouds are far to sea this day.
The birds ride upon currents of air sculptured by the sun.
Petrels speak of gathering clouds and breaking surf.

Let us harken to their song.
To pursue our love before the rising of the cloud-swept moon.
It is the voice within that will not be silenced by our need.
Gulls now shout above the rising wind.

Within Desire

From the void we appear,
Naked and alone.

Afraid of that which is and what is to be.
Longing for that not yet defined.

Then you appear,
A sun among the stars.

You reach for me within the night.
The warmth of your touch defines the meaning sought within.

Desire fulfilled within an earthly Eden.
An embrace that illuminates the new moon sky.

Our journey swift and sure.
My longings fulfilled by your embrace.
For having loved, we are cast among the stars.

A Quiet Moment

I have sought the quiet,
A moment of reflection.
Company of solitude and singing bird.

A dream cast like a fly into the stream.
To catch but a fantasy of thought.
A dream then lifted from roaring water.

Solitude does not exist.
The past, the future does intrude.
Memories awaken as slumber is sought.

You are with me now.
A presence dwelling in both sun and shadow.
A voice now made from flowing water.

Be bold to sit beside me.
Tempt me to hold your hand.
The presence of a dream now found.

Awaiting

What is love but waiting?
A glance returned among a crowd.
A smile of desire's recognition.

To wait for that not seen yet felt within.
A meeting, a glass of wine,
Perchance to hold then sleep.

Is not the heart a voyage?
Forever anticipating
Fulfillment in a dream.

To return once more to that not seen,
A glance, a smile.
Anticipation far greater than what is found.

A Painting

Do not dwell within a painting.
Step forth from poppies and fields of wheat.

Can I love that which does not exist?
Forever a moment painted in time.

In loneliness I seek you.
Yet you dwell within the canvas upon my wall.

A creation of the artist mind.
A reflection of needs unmet.

Yet within my chamber I recline.
To admire that which I love but cannot hold.

The Warmth of You

No stranger to the winter chill am I.
I can endure the cold when you are near.

The first moments within the bed.
Cold sheets and homemade quilts.

Then you touch me and I am warm again.
Your body caresses me in a most gentle way.

The covers about our heads
Keep the chill of winter from our breaths.
How warm you are when wintry guest seek entrance within.

Wondrous night when cold wind blows.
Your warmth against me within the feather bed.

A Gentle Rain

Music cascades about me.
It falls like water that absolves me.
My sins cleansed by rhythm and beat.

At first a gentle rain.
Then thunder excites the sky
The rain seeks entrance within my room.

A Chopin melody is played upon tin.
A crescendo of thunder
Then an adagio of soft rain falls anew.

From the meadow a wild bird calls.
To build the nest and feed the young
The lark is not alone as I in morning light.

Shall not regrets be so resolved?
Can I not feel both rain and music entwined?
Am I so lost that within solitude I must remain?

Phantom Lover

In a chamber I dwell in solitude.
Upon the settee I sit in rigid pose.
Unread books and papers tossed.

Can a phantom be created from thought alone?
A being of dream and awakened thought.
Revealed by sunlight upon leaves
Or hidden by shadows within the grove.

I seek you in the night and in the mist of morning light.
Do you stroll in a garden where flowers breathe and nectar awaits?
Perchance to amble upon a deserted beach?

Perhaps it is only memories now lost that I seek.
Dreams that vanish too quickly in the dawn.
Pain that does not cease, until I embrace you within my solitude.

The Future

"What future?" I shout aloud.
I only dwell in that now seen.
Voices, not echoes from the past, are heard by me.

Yet you dwell within me, like the soul of man.
Who am I that I should see a future void of you?
The past matures within me now.

All else I have cast aside for your love.
Others trodden underfoot like chaff beneath the miller's wheel.
That which remains in purest form is only you.

Can there be a future without desire?
An emptiness where love does not dwell.
I seek you within the shelter of a dream.

To the floor I do fall unheard.
Too close to hell to believe in heaven.
The summer breeze blows and scent of gardenias fill the night.

I am alone yet you speak and are heard.
To seek you in the darkened room,
Your image in a shroud of moonlight now seen.

The Drive-In and the Mosquito

A Studebaker and popcorn night.
Rolled-up jeans with exaggerated cuffs.

Dollar night to fill a car.
The menu but a concession stand delights.

Freckles and unkempt hair.
How beautiful you are on a summer eve.

The Goddess of the Hunt arises to salute your loveliness.
Fireflies and moon glow hover about you
Like guardian angels unseen.

Top down we sit as travelers amongst the stars.
Awaiting the main feature like an opening prayer.

About our legs the hunters of the night appear.
Humming summer's timeless tune.

Youthful promises made to love beyond the summer moon.
Silent prayers unspoken, yet heard aloud within the heart.

Awake My Love

Awake my love who sleeps upon my breast.
It is but a gentle rain that lulls you into drowsy repose.

Do you not hear the meadow's call or the roar of the brook?
Wildflowers gather the morning dew yet you sleep.

I smell the breath of roses and gardenias from within the stone wall.
The moments of youth too swiftly flee
Like summer clouds before the wind.

The moon now seeks the gentle west where it shall sleep alone.
Are you more the daughter of the moon or the sun's fair nymph?

You lie there unaware of my most gently gaze.
I look upon the wildflower hues of your hair.

Sleep on so soundly that I remain a silent witness
Transfixed by beauty.
Afraid to touch so fair a dream.

The Aran Islands

Stone that seeks the sky above the sea.
Sentinels that guard Ireland's western shore.

Cliffs that rise from the ocean's grasp
Stone to be pounded to sand by unrepentant Atlantic swell.

The language of falling surf and petrel call.
Spoken to Irish and Viking souls alike.

Do dreams cease where no land remains?
Look beyond the land to the colors of sky and sea.

The sunset of a painter's brush.
A rising moon, a poet's verse.

West Indies

Do not the hips sway to the calypso beat?
Desire's fulfillment should we meet.

Eyes search the wandering crowd.
Tourist or native of no concern
When drums of goat hide and tin are beaten.

Rainbows are worn by the sea like the feathers of a cockatoo's dress.
An island of celestial promise awaits the dreamer's brush.

What drink shall I toast the warming sun
That bathes your skin in light?
A funky monkey or a shot of rum.

My mind is clear, nourished by Corona and a twist of lime.
Pagan thoughts now released.

I shall ask your name when the coffee is served.
A solitary night with you was not enough.

A firm embrace, a stranger's scent.
Illusions of love abound in a tropic night.

Yes, it is time to drink more rum.
Then when morning comes, I will know what I have done.

Waiting

Have I not waited for you as seasons changed?
The fields of yellows now turned to burnt orange and scarlet red.
Clouds race southeast with the call of geese.

Life is but waiting for a season's change.
The thawing of the brook.
The softening of ice upon the eves.

How long must I wait to know?
Love remains within the heart unheard.
Does not discontent come when alone?

I await your image, your voice.
A text not answered; no reply to my call.
Thoughts now empty yet anticipation remains within my thought.

To whom shall I write?
Who will call my name when flowers bloom once more?
Questions are but riddles waiting to be solved.

Vanishing Images

Upon the table a Polaroid image is placed.
Too soon your smile fades from my view
Boxes of unshared dreams await within the hall.

What shall I do when alone I pace about the room?
Silent within a thought where laughter once prevailed.
Touching yet unfelt.

Too swiftly thoughts depart.
A voice, a sigh, a thought is lost.
Only fading images remain

A Tropic Night

Alone where warm seas flow.
Hibiscus and bougainvillea adorn the gentle breeze in sweet perfume.

The ocean swell embraces the jagged coral.
Moonlight plays upon the salty foam.

Our feet warmed by burning wood.
Flames rise to end in meteorite splendor on a starry night.

Laughter and song mixed with a warm margarita.
Should these moments not last
Until the sun paints the ocean a reddish glow?

Sleep now in the fold of my arms.
Moments of a tropic night, too soon to sleep in the dawn

The Problem of Being Southern

Who am I that I should write a verse?
My roots untraceable.
A history unknown.

A pride now lost, not to be found.
Others know their father's land.
Unlike Ulysses, I have no home, no city state.

A part of this; a part of that.
My father Irish, English or a mix.
No land now claims his past or mine.

I am a descendent of the unknown.
Roots no deeper than a century's tale.
Blown by changing winds to wars not won.

A stone without a verse.
A member of the universal mix.
A traveler who searches beneath a star unknown.

The Month That Should Not Be

There is a month that should not be.
August the child of summer heat.

Killing month that stalks my soul
Preys on both young and old.

War and peace it comes as a thief.
To take that which I now hold.

September a respite to provide.
October with changing leaf.

August is an ending not sought.
A summer's dream lost to me.

The earth dries and waits.
Summer clouds do not speak.

A dry wind and cicada call.
A month that takes, and does not yield to prayer alone.

Have I Not Called Your Name?

In the night, the clock speaks in solitude.
My eyes trace the outline of a moonlit room.

I would for even a trace of you now.
A visage of a smile; the fading candle's flame.

Images appear in half-light.
Silhouettes that haunt me in the silent night

Unreal like thoughts of you.
Touching yet not seen.

We have followed the natural rhythm.
Time obedient to nature's law.

Can I find solace in this night of tossing.
Your scent lingers upon the summer air.

You cannot return to me.
I go to you in thought as the morning dove awakens.

The Touch of You

I did not think it possible to love you more
The foolishness of youth looked not beyond today.

Each year I find that only love for you exist.
You nourish me like the brook the meadow's song.

The touch of you when first we awake in morning light.
To know that I live only in your embrace.

Kiss me now for time is not obedient to my command.
Too soon my strength will yield to the rule of natural law.

Should your love cease upon a winter's morn,
To awaken without your touch, afraid and alone.

My world would be:
An earth without light, a dawn without the brightness of a star.

An Innocent Glance

I had come to read at the Moulin café
To taste the wine and to be alone.

A book of poetic verse.
My companion unread upon the table lay.

A distant violin plays a song unknown to me.
A musical afternoon now spent in the warmth of the sun

Then about me I did look.
You were there unknown to me.

In a distant stare we met but for a moment's glance.
Your eyes searched and found the void within.

To play with loneliness is unfair.
I would not protest any words you said.

Yet in this moment of solitude.
A glance from a stranger will do.

Perhaps another day, another hour,
A mutual smile to share.
'Perhaps' is a word well known to me.

The Seven Acts of Love

A child within the womb; a promise to fulfill.
Love unknown yet pulses within.
The warming seed within the land.

The schoolboy who saw you there beneath the oak.
Feelings stirred like wind from off the sea.
Unknown, unknowing yet you are there.

Romantic love driven by nature's force.
The clap of thunder, the rising swell of the sea.
Bare feet entwined in a warm lagoon.

The ambitious man who sought what could not be possessed.
No time for you or for me.
Profits to be made.

Retirement now and years yet to be.
Can peace be found when strife has ceased?
Perhaps we shall love again.

The aging of both mind and soul.
Yet restlessness stirs within.
To pursue you in dreams alone.

The ending as it were the beginning.
Innocence returns and peace within.
All is lost and found again.

The Seventh Day

The barren days that consume the week.
Monday a day of dread and solemn work.
Errands to run and workaday tasks abound.

Tuesday a resolution is made.
I shall laugh once more and call your name.
My mission, to fill the space of time to be.

Wednesday lives because of Friday's promise
Hopeful plan to be implemented.
A point of no return is found.

Thursday is an awakening to what may lay ahead.
Dreams while yet awake.
Per chance bright sun and beach sand.

Friday is a day of hope.
Perhaps to love again.
A street café and idle chatter with a friend.

Saturday is a day to sleep.
A call or a letter may arrive.
Desire and expectation embrace.

Sunday sulks with the morning paper.
Of all the measurements of time,
Sunday should be banned from every week.

The Gathering of Flowers

Have I not gathered flowers in the morning light?
In pastures dressed in yellow hues.
Across the fields marigolds sought.

Wildflowers cut to be arrayed.
Upon the table set.

The Land Sought

What is that land that I have sought?
Meadows and streams.
A warm friend to greet and to embrace.

A breaking dawn.
Clouds swept from the sea.
A morning kiss when first we see.

A child the echo of ourselves,
The sweet scent of newborn life.
A playful tune within my heart.

The Pond: Reflections of Myself

I measure the year by the unkempt pond.
Is not all of life more clearly seen in the reflection of water?

Those who drink from the surface of my pond are all invited guests.
There is life within untouched by me.
Concerts performed by frogs and chirping crickets.

In the early evening, the stage is lit by the lighting bugs fiery dance.
Set designs are soon altered by the seasons.
All seasons have their colors even the mossy green of winter.

Dangers abound around the pond.
The predatory cat sees not beauty but a feast of motion.
Driven by instinct, untamed it stalks
And soon plays with a fallen leaf.

I must admit that I built the pond, but I am not the keeper of it.
Its life comes from falling water and the sparkling sun.
Perhaps it is merriest of all when night falls
And the moon sails with canvas clouds.

Ideas flow like the windswept motions of the water.
I too am altered by the wind.
What I seek most is your reflection upon the surface of the pond.

The Soldier and the Sea

Bold green water strikes the shore with thrashing force,
Salty spray cast from rocks.
About the wet stone, shadows swim.

Dreams are dice cast to an angry sea.
A beach of sand, fragments of the past.
Bottles tossed carelessly to both ebb and flow of tides.

Wind whips the palm and lifts the gull.
Webfeet of sandpipers race the crab to its sandy den
A lover's hope abounds where land and sea entwine.

Are you next to me or far away?
Before us the moon rises above the Atlantic swell.
Will you watch for me when dawn breaks in weave of scarlet cloud?

In a desert far away, I too dream beneath the rising of a moon.
I know not if fate will shout or in silence be announced.
It is a sea dream that sustains me now, alone and afraid.

Afternoon Affair

Hawaii is Eden's taste.
Drinks prepared in the sun.
Falling breakers shatter against the reef of coral.

Alone you sit, a sacrament to desire.
Lips to tempt then teach
Paddle fans and fragrant sheets

Bed cooled by trade-wind breeze.
Scents of orchids and Bougainville.
Gauguin painting slightly tilted.

To write, to call, to text.
Promises made not to keep.
The Tropic of Cancer ignites the animal within.

SNIPPETS
OF THOUGHTS

A Journey from Myself

Why do I travel to different shores
or stroll solitarily along a lane of trees
Soon to be changed to burning flame
by autumn winds and frigid nights?

I often ask myself what have I gained
in the pursuit beyond my room?
The answer is very clear,
it is the journey from myself that I have sought.

The Impressionist

A journey to Paris, a whimsical thought indeed.
Was it not December and the probability of rain?

"This is not art but a child's painting,"
a critic was heard to say as he stood before a Monet.
With a frown, I replied, "Are impressions ever complete?"

The Lurking Spellchecker

Technology is a very dangerous overseer.
The lurking spellchecker is the voyeur of my dreams.

When I meant to spell "Flash Gordon,"
it corrected itself to "Flesh Garden."
I don't think that there is a need to google that.

A staff member named Chris did not realize
that his salutation had been automatically changed to Christ.
We often waited for the lord's reply.

Can I blame the folly of errors upon that unseen?
Perhaps if I read what I wrote before I sent,
I could avoid the voyeur of my thoughts.

An Author Without a Reader

I have often thought that the best place to hide a thought
is on the Internet.

That world of indifference
is ignored by both friend and stranger.

A Facebook Friend

I have often thought, do you really exist?
An image uploaded of yourself.

Words that please an audience of one.
Unread, yet praised by another.

The Reader

Of what interest to others can I be?
My words searched by those unknown to me.
What is written is stored, analyzed and then forgotten.

ABOUT THE AUTHOR

Franklin Lafayette King was born in the Panhandle of Texas and spent much of his youth on the Blackland Prairie. He received a commission through the University of Texas in Austin and soon became involved in the Vietnam Conflict. After additional academic preparation, he moved to the foothills of the Appalachians. In addition to combat, he experienced both the eyes of a hurricane and an F-4 tornado, events that were to influence much of his later work.